"Since none of us are sleeping together—yet—let's have a drink and talk about sex."

Poe cast a wicked look around the table. Sydney could feel the sexual tension hum amongst the group, but particularly between herself and Ray. And so she wasn't surprised when Poe grinned and said, "Truth or Dare."

Sydney leveled her gaze at Ray. "I'm game." From what she could see smoldering in Ray's eyes as they met hers, he understood her double meaning and was game, as well. *For more than Truth or Dare.*

Lauren downed a shot of whiskey. "Fine. I'm in, too."

"All right," Doug said, clapping his hands together. He high-fived Jess and Anton while Kinsey toasted the other women.

"Then sex it is." Poe paused for effect. "Sydney. Truth or Dare? I'm curious to know if you orgasmed the first time you had sex."

Heat began to spread down Sydney's body at the memory of that long, hot night with Ray so many years ago. This was exactly what she needed to work out of her system—the unbelievable sex they'd had. The kind of sex she was sure they'd have again before they left this island....

Dear Reader,

Writing romance is a dream come true, a fantasy, if you will. Imagine living vicariously through fictional characters—dream jobs...dream vacations...dream lovers. It's all there.

My gIRL-gEAR series for Harlequin Blaze has also been a dream to write. I have lived with these characters for months, their likenesses hanging on a bulletin board in my bedroom office. They have inhabited every aspect of my life, including a year's worth of lunch hours. It's going to be hard to say goodbye. The pictures will be coming down, much to my husband's relief...but only until the next story's characters go up to replace them. (Sorry, sweetie!)

And drop me a line at alison@alisonkent.com if the girls of gIRL-gEAR have made their way into your heart—the way best friends should do!

Best,

Alison Kent

P.S. Please stop by www.girl-gear.com and visit. Yes, it really does exist!

Books by Alison Kent

HARLEQUIN BLAZE
24—ALL TIED UP
32—NO STRINGS ATTACHED

HARLEQUIN TEMPTATION
594—CALL ME
623—THE HEARTBREAK KID
664—THE GRINCH MAKES GOOD
741—THE BADGE AND THE BABY
750—FOUR MEN & A LADY

BOUND TO HAPPEN

Alison Kent

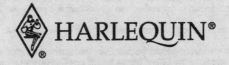

HARLEQUIN®

TORONTO • NEW YORK • LONDON
AMSTERDAM • PARIS • SYDNEY • HAMBURG
STOCKHOLM • ATHENS • TOKYO • MILAN • MADRID
PRAGUE • WARSAW • BUDAPEST • AUCKLAND

(Alphabetically—because it's only fair!)
To Vicia Collins, Jennifer Harbour, Annette John,
Carolyn Taflinger. Thanks to your friendship,
I've survived the last 13 years....
But PLEASE don't make me stay for 13 more!
There are so many things I could say, but I'll only say one.
"I like your hair!"

ISBN 0-373-79044-9

BOUND TO HAPPEN

Prologue

The gIRLS behind gIRL-gEAR
by Samantha Venus for *Urban Attitude Magazine*

Here we are once again, dear reader, checking in on our gIRLS. (Excuse me, our women.) It seems your intrepid reporter is inches away from the bottom of what is going on with Lauren Hollister and that sexy Anton Neville. Could it be we are about to learn that love at first sight is a tad overrated?

And speaking of firsts, my sources tell me that gIRL-gEAR's CEO, Sydney Ford, has spent her summer vacation with the object of her very first schoolgirl crush. (Who's walking whose plank, anyway?) And isn't *that* a romantic blast from the past!

Yes, friends, it would have been just that, had their vacation cruise not turned into a vacation disaster. (Though we here at *Urban Attitude* do not gET how anyone can call a week on a tropical island with a veritable menu of beefcake disastrous.) Oh, did we neglect to mention they sailed away on the *Indiscreet?*

Inside this issue you will find the complete *scoopage* on both Ms. Ford's and Ms. Hollister's tropical trysts and treats, as well as tips for the ultimate in nude sunbathing! See an exclusive excerpt available online at www.girlgear.com.

1

IN A PERFECT WORLD, thought Sydney Ford, she would plan the most magnificent summer vacation.

She would make her own travel arrangements. She loved the idea of seeing the country by train. She would book her own accommodations. She liked to be pampered, unapologetically so. She would choose her own traveling companion. She longed to share a relaxing week with one of her very best friends.

But the world was not perfect.

Her summer vacation was turning out to be less than magnificent. And she had no one to blame but herself.

Months ago, for some remarkably harebrained reason, she'd had the bright idea to offer a sailing trip on her father's soon-to-be-sold yacht to the winner of the experimental scavenger hunt organized by gIRL-gEAR.com's editor, Macy Webb. Knowing the Web site's gIRL gAMES column would benefit from Macy's test group's enthusiasm, Sydney, as gIRL-gEAR CEO, had felt the high-stakes offer made for a savvy business proposition.

One of their mutual friends, Ray Coffey, had won.

And now here Sydney stood, stranded on a Caribbean island, well aware that complaining only served to give her situation a "poor little rich girl" sting.

What work-weary single career woman wouldn't want to be stranded on a Caribbean island? A private island at that. With a tropical beachfront villa outfitted to sleep ten, a live-in staff and four servings of beefcake among her fellow castaways.

Me, me, me, Sydney wanted to shout. But she sighed, instead, and boosted a hip onto the foot-wide wooden railing of the villa's first-floor wraparound veranda. A soft evening breeze sifted through her hair and she tucked loose strands behind her ear, inhaling the clean salty essence of the sea.

The sunset was spectacular. She'd never seen a sunset here that wasn't. Tonight, wispy clouds floated on a palette of soft pastels, though Sydney knew well the intense beauty of sunsets born in fire. The beach was equally amazing—the sand eggshell white, the water the tropical green-tinged blue never found along the Texas Gulf coast.

But even better than the view of the sky and the surf was the view of the three men standing at the shoreline, ankle-deep in the water and staring out to sea. Actually, Sydney mused, they were more than likely staring at the catamaran sailing by several miles off the coast. But she was in a contemplative mood and, therefore, allowed to project.

Each man was similarly dressed. Doug Storey wore navy board shorts with a white-and-gray hibiscus print. Anton Neville's trunks were of the same cut, but colored in turquoise and hot-island red. Both Doug and Anton were tall with lanky swimmers' physiques. Anton's blond hair was a riot of curls. Doug's, a shade darker, was longer, looser, inviting the touch of a woman's hands. But it was the last man, the third man, who commanded Sydney's attention.

Ray Coffey was a big man and beautifully built. The trunks he wore hit him at the knee and were a bright beach yellow with a black piping trim. The vivid color was the perfect contrast for his olive-hued complexion. His brown hair was the color of espresso, rich and thick and cut to fall softly over his brow, his eyes a dark emerald-green. Even from here Sydney could see the way the ocean breeze threaded like a lover's fingers through the strands. She wondered what time had made of the texture. She wondered what else about him time might have changed.

Sitting on the veranda, she drew her knees to her chest and wrapped her arms around her shins. Her brown-and-gold tribal-print sarong fell open, catching on the shrubbery tucked close to the villa and revealing her leg and hip and the edge of her butter-colored bikini bottoms. A softer hue than the yellow Ray wore. But still, yellow. *Like Ray wore.* The similarity struck her for some strange reason. Especially since she was too practical to believe in intangible, nebulous signs.

The light from the setting sun silhouetted his body, accentuating the breadth of his shoulders and, when he turned to the side… Sydney's breath caught. Not unexpectedly, but with a sharp visceral hitch that broke her rhythm. Yet, try as she might, she could find no logical explanation for her unusually fierce physical response to Ray. This overreaction had to be an aberration, the island casting a sensual spell. Nothing else came close to making sense.

She wasn't a stranger to the male body. She wasn't, in fact, a stranger to Ray's. But eight years had passed since she'd known his touch. And eight years meant added definition to the muscles of his chest, a chiseled distinction to his abs. Eight years had also thickened the whorls of hair growing low on his belly as well as, no doubt, the nest of hair cushioning his sex.

His trunks rode low on his hips and, standing as he was in profile, Sydney's gaze was drawn to his flat stomach, his waistband and the impressive bulge beneath. Her imagination followed her wandering eyes and she took a deep breath, unnerved by the way her heart beat like a bass drum in her chest. She stretched out her legs along the railing, crossed her ankles, letting her head fall back to rest against one of the veranda's support beams.

A relentless tingle settled unmercifully in the core of her belly. She squeezed her legs together and smoothed her palms down the length of her thighs. Even the feel of her own hands caressing her limbs failed to calm her and did, in fact, heighten the sensations simmering beneath the surface of her skin.

Since Ray had reentered her life, unnerved was not an uncommon state in which to find her emotions, just as aroused was not an unusual condition in which to find her body. Neither were comfortable situations. Both she intended to address during the days of this vacation. She had to get him out of her system before they returned to the States.

This obsessive infatuation was beginning to take its toll; her daydreams had recently crossed the line into erotic fantasy, cutting into her concentration in such a way that she feared her work might suffer. She couldn't allow any relationship, whether one of her imagination's making or one from the past, to color the business decisions or personal choices she made.

Especially after having seen that very thing happen with her father. She refused to sink to his level of disloyalty—to her business, to her friends or to herself—and was willing to do anything, *anything* to make sure it didn't happen. Ray Coffey was becoming the sort of consuming distraction her life didn't need. Which meant it was time to prove to herself that he wasn't the lover her memory declared him to be.

This trip had originally been planned to last just over a week and a half. With the *Indiscreet* docked in Belize City in preparation for its imminent sale, Ray had arranged with the two-person crew for the fifty-seven-foot yacht to circle the western Caribbean, slowly exploring the barrier reef along the coast of Belize before making stops in Jamaica and the Caymans on the return.

In addition to the travel plans, the vacation invitations had been left up to Ray. He'd asked both Anton and Doug to come along, as he was in negotiations with their architectural firm, Neville and Storey, and the trip made for good business, as well as a good time. He'd also asked Jess Morgan, another friend from his core circle of six, all of whom played together on the same adult soccer league.

And then he'd invited Sydney.

She'd been more than tempted—by the trip, yes. Until last year's falling-out with her father, Nolan, she'd never turned him down when he'd asked her to go sailing. But she'd also been tempted by the prospect of being confined with Ray on the *Indiscreet*. An intimately innocent confinement, where running from their mutual attraction would mean a trip to the bottom of the sea.

So she'd given him a conditional yes and then invited her three conditions.

Because the six gIRL-gEAR partners were discussing a possible change to the firm's corporate structure, Sydney had asked Annabel Lee to come along. Annabel, known around the office as Poe, had moved up rapidly through company ranks. She was currently under consideration to replace Chloe Zuniga as vice president of cosmetics and accessories once Chloe launched the new gUIDANCE gIRL mentoring program. Chloe had assured the others that Poe was not the fire-breathing dragon she seemed.

And getting to know Poe away from the office, woman-to-woman, was Sydney's prime plan.

She'd also invited Lauren Hollister and had done so for two reasons—one obvious, one personal. The first was Ray's invitation to Anton Neville. After a year in an exclusive relationship, Lauren and Anton had recently split, though it was clear to all their friends that the two were more miserable apart than they'd ever been together.

Matchmaking always had the potential to backfire, but in this case Sydney was willing to take the chance. Lauren was one of Sydney's gIRL-gEAR partners and she had to consider the company's well-being, as well as that of her friend. And lately Lauren had been coming to work in body only, leaving her enthusiasm and concentration behind.

But when it came to Lauren, Sydney had an additional consideration. And that was the friendship blossoming between her father and Lauren. The two had been seeing too much of one another for Sydney's peace of mind. As angry as she was with Nolan, she did love him, and the last thing he needed in his life was another creative, volatile woman. Or an impulsive fling.

Finally, Sydney had coaxed Kinsey Gray into coming along. Kinsey had been a marketing major and had shared several of Sydney's classes at University of Texas. Now the VP of the company's sportswear and party-wear divisions, Kinsey had an innate intuition when it came to trends, an uncanny sense of fashion and a slightly offbeat way of looking at the world, which Sydney felt would be a welcome relief to the trip's inevitable tension.

The tension had begun immediately.

The group of eight vacationers had never made it farther than twelve miles before the *Indiscreet* developed a problem with its hydraulics. Convenient, actually, that twelve miles, because, before the crew nursed the limping ketch back to Belize City for repairs, Sydney and the others had loaded their supplies into the onboard aluminum dinghy and moved their vacation from yacht to island. Specifically, Coconut Caye, the private twelve-acre island Sydney's father owned.

Coconut Caye had always been the first planned stop on their itinerary. But it hadn't been intended as their final—or only—destination. Again Sydney realized she had nothing to complain about. The island was the epitome of paradise. Looking ahead, she had several days to spend doing nothing more than swimming, snorkeling and sunbathing.

And now that she thought about it rationally, logically, instead of with the irritation she'd felt this morning when the *Indiscreet* had given up the ghost, the change of plans might work to her advantage. The island offered more privacy than she would ever have found on the yacht. And privacy would play nicely into her plans to seduce Ray Coffey. Suddenly, Sydney realized, this adventure held more promise than she'd originally thought when forced to relocate earlier today.

She turned her attention back to the beach, where the three men were now engaged in a round of extreme Frisbee among the coconut palms. She had a dozen other things she could be doing; beach Frisbee was not exactly a spectator sport. Yet, try as she might, she couldn't tear her gaze from Ray.

He dived to catch Anton's toss, and Sydney drank in the intoxicating visual. Ray's long torso extended, delineating his rib cage and hair-dusted pectorals, emphasizing the length of his scar. His reaching arm stretched, beautifully elongating his biceps and forearms. She took in the spread of his fingers when he palmed the Frisbee down to the sand.

Blood surged through Sydney until her nerves hummed wildly from fingers to toes. She wanted him in ways she found surprising. Physical ways that had never been a part of her experience, yet lived vividly in her fantasies. Since his return to Houston late last year, Ray had made it more than clear that the attraction remained mutual, which made Sydney laugh. They'd been so young and innocent that first time....

Sensing movement at her side, she looked up to see she'd been joined on the veranda by Poe, wearing a pair of plain black sarong pants tied well below her waist. Her matching triangle bikini top left little of her porcelain curves to the imagination. She also wore a look of disgust that pulled Sydney's attention from the beach. "Are you okay?"

"In what context?" Poe asked, dusting her hands together as if to rid them of something unpleasant. "Medically? Financially? Socially?"

Sydney couldn't help appreciating her co-worker's theatrical flair. Or her predicament. "In this situation? Socially, for sure."

Poe rolled her eyes. Irises of near black and a slight almond slant to her lids emphasized her exotic Asian-American looks, as did the slashed angles and layers of hair framing her cheekbones. "Considering I was so looking forward to this trip, I can't believe I'm saying this, but…"

She ruffled both hands through her hair and lifted her chin. "I am thrilled beyond belief to be ship-wrecked. We would no doubt have ended up at the bottom of the sea, anyway, once we factored in the weight of the eggshells."

"Eggshells?" Sydney asked with a frown.

Poe's elegant brows shot up archly. "To walk on? Don't tell me you thought fifty-seven feet would be enough room for Lauren and Anton's emotional baggage. From what I've seen so far, even your father's twelve acres might be a tight fit."

Sydney felt a sharp pang of guilt. She hadn't thought the ex-lovers would start tossing verbal barbs the minute the group set sail. And the fact that Anton had been seeing Poe on a casual basis had never factored into Sydney's decision to invite both women— which it apparently should have. Nothing serious was going on between the two, as everyone but Lauren seemed to know.

"Where is Lauren, anyway?" Sydney asked.

Poe gave a sideways tip of her head. "She's in the kitchen with Kinsey and Jess. They're working on…dinner."

"Great. I'm starving."

This time Poe took a moment to apparently weigh

her appetite against the kitchen skills of the temporary help. "Tell me again what's happening with the staff? I saw their boat leave earlier, but I was on the *Indiscreet* packing my things, so I never did hear for sure what was going on."

Sydney nodded, then indulged in a private smile. Neither Poe nor any of the guests needed to worry about the quality of the meals after this evening's. "The Duartes. Auralie and Menga. They weren't expecting us to be here but for the one day and had only stocked limited provisions. When they found out we'd be staying, they had to make a trip to the mainland for supplies. They'll be back tomorrow."

Swinging her legs down from the railing, Sydney got to her feet, settling automatically into the role of hostess, which she'd acted here for Nolan so many times. "Wait until you see what Auralie can do with tomatoes, roasted chicken and black beans. Unbelievable."

Poe cast a wistful glance at her audibly protesting stomach. "I was hoping to eat before tomorrow."

"I don't know about Lauren or Jess, but Kinsey's a decent cook. And if we hurry, we can stop any disaster in the making."

"If it's all the same to you, I'd just as soon stay out of the kitchen." Poe dug in her heels. "I'm afraid I'm on Lauren's hit list, and I've learned to be picky about who I let shoot me down."

Sydney threaded her hands through her hair and fluffed. This fiasco she'd created was rocketing out of control. The time had come to play peacemaker— though she had to admit that spending her vacation in mediation held zero appeal.

There were times she wished she'd inherited less

of her father's mind for negotiation and more of her mother's in-your-face style. This was one of those times. "Well, then. We'll just have to trust those three with dinner, won't we? As scary a thought as that may be."

"Scary isn't the half of it," Poe said with a huff.

"Dinner will be fine." Sydney adjusted the knot of her sarong. "If not, we can dig into my stash of Rice Krispies treats."

"And for the next ten days?"

"We'll have to ration."

Poe shook her head and moved her hands to her hips. "Not the food. The tension."

Sydney studied the other woman's wits-end demeanor, sympathizing with Poe's uncomfortable plight. "You're talking about the tension between Lauren and Anton."

"Between Lauren and Anton. Between Lauren and me. I haven't had a true, nonworking vacation in years. And I am not about to have this one ruined by this unresolved thing between those two." Poe looked out toward the beach where the game of Frisbee was still going on.

Then she looked back at Sydney and shrugged. "Anton and I are friends, that's it. But if I'm going to be tried and convicted of being more, then why shouldn't I reap the obvious fruits of committing the crime? It's not like he's the least bit hard on the eyes."

Anton *was* totally gorgeous, Sydney had to agree. But she was also quite sure Poe was perfectly capable of answering her own question. "I think we both know you don't have it in you to hurt Lauren that way."

Poe blew out an inelegant snort. "Too bad the reverse isn't true."

Sydney's mouth twisted. "Lauren's just overly sensitive when it comes to Anton. I doubt she has anything against you personally."

"Well, either she wants to be with Anton or she doesn't. She's trying hard to have it both ways, and it's hardly fair to the rest of us. I mean, look out there." Poe lifted her chin, indicating the human scenery—three men whipping the Frisbee across the beach. "Tell me what you see."

What Sydney saw was more than Poe could imagine. Images that even Sydney wasn't sure were memories or the creative workings of her mind. And none of her thoughts were anything she wanted to explain or to share. Not with Poe. Not with anyone.

Ray was her fantasy, her mind-candy, as were her plans for his seduction. "Well, I see an absolutely gorgeous tropical sunset. I see a postcard-worthy scene of palm trees and rippling waves and a beach clean enough to eat off. But I have a feeling you're talking about Anton, Doug and Ray."

"Exactly." Poe moved closer to the veranda railing, hitched one hip onto the edge. "Three very appealing possibilities for an exciting vacation fling."

Sydney had already narrowed her own possibilities down to one. And she had matchmaking plans for a second. Which left Poe only two choices. "You're forgetting about Jess."

Poe shook her head. "Not really. I know Anton is off-limits. And as much as it pains me to admit it, I also accept that the fling possibilities will have to be shared."

"How generous of you," Sydney replied, working hard to keep a straight face.

"My generosity is limited, trust me. If Lauren blows this chance, I *will* take full advantage when we get back to the States."

"Then we'll just have to make sure she doesn't blow anything, won't we."

"Taking matters into your own hands?" Poe asked, sliding a sly, sideways glance at Sydney.

Sydney lifted one shoulder and casually replied, "I'm thinking about it."

"Well, while you're thinking, I believe I will go ahead and give Lauren the wake-up call she needs." Poe hopped back to her feet. "Unless you have an objection?"

Back home in Houston, with gIRL-gEAR business at stake, Sydney would have more reasons to possibly object. But here and now? Even an unearthly intervention would be welcome. "Will you do me the favor of warning me in advance?"

Poe chuckled. "Consider yourself warned."

"Fair enough." Sydney linked her arm through Poe's. "Now let me show you the sundeck before it's too dark to get the full effect. I've never found a better place to sunbathe."

The fact that she sunbathed in the nude, Sydney kept to herself. It was a private indulgence she preferred not to share...though there was a man who'd once coaxed her to admit to the habit. She took one last look toward the beefcake on the beach and her hunger stirred. Dinner first. She'd get back to her plans for seducing Ray Coffey soon enough.

RAY TWIRLED the Frisbee on one index finger, listening with half an ear while Anton and Doug, standing three feet away, talked shop. Knowing full well that Sydney sat on the veranda watching the beach play, her long legs and a whole lot more of her gorgeous body exposed, made it difficult for him to keep his eye on the ball. Or, in this case, on the Frisbee.

When he'd won the sailing trip four months ago, he'd known immediately that he wanted Sydney along for the cruise. Hell, his fantasy had started the month before he'd won, when she'd first announced the use of her father's yacht as the prize for sticking out that ridiculous scavenger hunt. He'd determined that night that he was going to win and spend the week at sea letting Sydney walk his plank.

The stakes had been sweetened when they'd actually been paired up for the hunt and he'd been assigned to discover a list of her deepest, darkest secrets. At that point, the game itself had become the prize, the cruise just a sweet little extra. He'd thought for a couple of months about keeping the guest list that simple. Him and Sydney. The two of them alone, but for the yacht's minimal crew. Life at its absolute intimate finest.

And then he woke up.

Having Sydney all to himself was his fantasy, not hers. At least, he hadn't had any vibes saying differently. Since he'd transferred to the Houston Fire Department, in fact, after five years working out of College Station with the Texas Task Force One on urban search and rescue, the only concentrated time they'd had together had been the give-and-take dinner dates devoted to the scavenger hunt.

Ray wasn't complaining. At least not about that. For one thing, he'd learned enough about her by coaxing her into revealing the details he needed to know to win this trip. And even if their dates had been all about the hunt, they'd given him more one-on-one time with Sydney than he'd ever had—with his clothes on, anyway. No, his complaints were more about the things he hadn't learned. Things he was bound and determined to find out before they returned home to Texas.

She'd been a year behind him in high school, in his brother Patrick's class. Yet she'd always seemed years older than the girls his age, the girls he'd dated, even the girls who'd…taken him under their wing during his first year at Texas A&M. And he'd found himself making comparisons, which made no sense, because except for that one time, they'd known each other only casually.

Off to Ray's side, Doug and Anton continued to discuss developmental possibilities for a new property they'd acquired. Ray continued to feign interest. The sun had reached the edge of the horizon, putting an end to their game and ringing his internal dinner bell. His hunger roused, he glanced again toward the villa, watching as Sydney moved from the veranda railing to her feet.

She was a tall woman, with long limbs that Ray knew fit nicely around his own larger body. Or had nicely fit eight years ago. He'd bulked up since then. And he wasn't the only one with a body developed by time and working out. Sydney was slender, but not skinny, and had filled out beautifully since his hands had last explored the budding fullness of her curves. The strapless bandeau tube wrapped around her chest hugged her breasts like a soft yellow skin, and his palms itched to skate over the surface, to feel the taut press of her nipples.

When she lifted her arms to run her hands through her hair, exposing both her stomach's smooth skin and the knot of her sarong riding low on her belly, he barely suppressed a rising groan. When she turned away, giving him a clear view of the strong lines of her back and her narrow waist easily spanned by his hands, he dug his toes into the sand. When she hooked her arm through Poe's and started to walk away, the sarong snugged tight to her hips and caressing the tight swells of her backside, Ray dropped the Frisbee and looked down, working to catch his breath as hunger grabbed hard between his legs.

Their one night together had followed her high-school graduation and his first year of college, and it hadn't lasted long enough to be called an affair. But Ray wasn't sure it qualified as a one-night stand, either. If it had, surely those hours they'd spent tangled naked between the cheap sheets of an even cheaper motel-room bed wouldn't still linger the way they did in his mind.

They'd been lingering more than usual today since this vacation had become landlocked and since, every time he'd turned around, Sydney had shed more of her clothes. Having looked forward to the sailing trip now for four months, he was surprised he didn't feel more disappointment at the forced change of plans. He hadn't been onboard the *Indiscreet* long enough even to think about getting his sea legs. Which proved he was more interested in the company than in the cruise.

Following Anton and Doug as they headed toward the villa in response to Lauren's call to, "Come and get it!", Ray knew he'd be a fool not to take advantage of an opportunity he'd never see again. Sydney had nowhere to run, nowhere to hide, nowhere to be for the next ten days, while he had the luxurious warmth of the sun, the seductive lure of the sea and the lush tropical nights in his favor.

He wasn't looking for happily-ever-after. He was only looking for answers, and whatever good time they might mutually share. In his line of work, he saw too much tragedy, too many families torn apart by accidents and disaster, both natural and man-made. His own family was no exception, irreparably damaged by his brother's still-unsolved disappearance three years ago in this very part of the world.

With the chances Ray took on the job, with the risky situations he encountered, he'd be stupid—and selfish—to consider any romantic involvement, to subject a partner to the very real possibility that he might lose his life on the job. He didn't have it in him to give Sydney or any woman a long-term promise, for her sake, as well as his own. Not when life was so fragile. Not when the loss of Patrick had shown him the truth of personal suffering for those left behind.

And he sure didn't have to involve his heart to enjoy his time here with Sydney. He knew that for certain. He'd been her first lover, a fact he hadn't appreciated fully at the time. He'd had his hands too full of her body to question his luck or her decision. But before they returned to the States, he intended to get the answers he needed about that night. Like why she hadn't returned his phone calls afterward. And why she'd haunted his memory ever since.

But most of all why, out of all the guys "Ice

Queen'' Sydney Ford had said no to, had she wrapped her arms around *his* neck and said yes.

DINNER THAT FIRST NIGHT at the villa on Coconut Caye was one of the more intense meals Ray remembered sitting through. The men, along with Poe and Kinsey, had carried the conversation, sharing tales of past vacations gone bad.

Among the six of them, they'd seen more than a few ports of call on more than a few continents and had faced lost luggage, mistaken identities and bungled reservations from car to hotel.

So far Lauren hadn't said a thing. She'd never even met Anton's gaze.

Sydney had talked, but not a lot, as if carefully weighing the import of what she had to say against the mystery of remaining silent. The mystery, of course, was all in Ray's mind, driven by her refusal to hold his gaze when their eyes met. Every time he glanced her way, he caught her staring. He even caught her looking back before he'd turned away.

Her expression teased him, the way she slowly lowered her lashes, the way her nostrils seemed to flare. The way her chin came up and her lips lightly parted. Even the way she lounged so casually, invitingly, one elbow braced on the chair back, her head propped in her hand, her crossed leg swinging with a motion that lifted, then lowered the gap in her sarong.

Ray couldn't decide if he was amused or intrigued. But he was definitely working on aroused, as he had been since they'd set sail this morning. Or, more accurately, as he had been every time they'd been in the same room since he'd introduced himself to her beneath the oak tree in Boom Daily's backyard eight long years ago.

There was just something about Sydney Ford that Ray couldn't get his mind around to figure out. The things he'd known about Sydney as a girl didn't mesh at all with what he'd learned recently from her father. Or what he knew about her as the CEO of gIRL-gEAR.

He wasn't sure the remaining days of this vacation would be enough time to reconcile his curiosity with the facts, but damned if he wouldn't be giving it his best shot, he mused. He forced his gaze from Sydney and back to the others as, one at a time, they finished up the meal of grilled steak and tossed salad put together at the last minute by Kinsey and Lauren, with questionable help from Jess.

Kinsey, at least, had no trouble making or maintaining eye contact with anyone at the table. And Poe—Poe had upped the stakes and was making contact with her body, Ray realized, as she got up to clear the table and leaned over Doug's shoulder to reach for an empty serving bowl.

Doug had pulled on a sleeveless shirt before sitting down to the impromptu dinner. Poe still wore her black bikini top. She brushed the barely covered swell of her breast against his barely covered shoulder. Ray couldn't say the move was made on purpose, but she didn't seem the least bit self-conscious about a touch that made Doug's eyes bulge.

In fact, now hugging the salad bowl to her middle, her hip cocked to the side, Poe glanced around the room with one brow arched and a twist to her mouth that Ray could've sworn meant trouble in paradise. Leaning into the forearm he'd braced on the table, he toyed with his steak knife, swirling the pointed tip in the sauce on his plate, smiling as he waited to find out exactly what she was up to. He didn't have to wait long.

"Is it just me," she said, looking from one man, one woman to the next, her dark eyes sparkling with indescribable mischief, "or do the rest of you get a sense that there is an unhealthy level of sexual tension in the air?"

After several silent seconds, Doug burst out laughing. Anton followed suit, snickering behind his hand, which had Lauren fuming and Sydney crossing her arms beneath her bandeau top and fighting to keep a straight face. All Ray could do was sit back and enjoy the show.

"At least it *appears* to be sexual." Poe gave a light shrug and started gathering up utensils. "I could be wrong, but I think the facts speak for themselves."

"Uh, Poe, what facts are you talking about?" Kinsey asked, prodding Jess's rib cage with her elbow and glaring when he leaned over and started breathing heavily into her ear. "Enough of that, mister. If I need heating up, I'll let you know."

Jess laughed. Sydney laughed. Even Poe laughed, this time leaning between Kinsey and Anton, giving Anton a dose of Doug's medicine while stacking the used dinner plates.

"The facts as I see them are that we're in the tropics, on a gorgeous island, surrounded by sand and surf, an incredible moonrise, a soft ocean breeze. And we're staring at each other and a table of dirty dishes when we could be having a lot of extracurricular fun."

With that, Poe headed for the kitchen—a huge

open-air affair separated from the main dining area by a wide serving bar—leaving the others speechless, but only for a second or two, then everyone started talking at once.

"Extracurricular works for me," Jess said, leaning in closer toward Kinsey again, nuzzling his face against her bare shoulder and making whimpering puppy-dog sounds.

Wearing a bright-red tank top with her khaki drawstring shorts, Kinsey patted his head accordingly. Then she threaded her fingers into his hair and used the hold to pull his head from her shoulder. Her smile was a show of bared teeth. "What part of 'enough' don't you understand?"

Jess sighed and slumped in his chair. "Does that mean extracurricular is out of the question?"

Eyes rolling, Kinsey could only shake her head. "You're hopeless and I give up."

Doug, being a guy, was more in tune with Jess's plight and told him so. "What it means, buddy, is that you'll have to take matters into your own hands."

A round of groans and cries of "Gross! Eww! Yuck!" went up from the women. Ray found himself chuckling under his breath. Then he found himself glancing at Sydney…and found her gaze focused on him. Not on Doug or on Kinsey or on Jess. Not even on Poe, whom Ray could hear rummaging around behind him in the kitchen cabinets.

No, Sydney was concentrating solely on him. And doing so with a look that wasn't the least bit shy or evasive. He would've said she was flirting, but her expression was hardly that simple. What he saw in her eyes was more of an invitation, a sultry temptation to join her in sin. Her blue eyes sparkled, her wide mouth offered him a private smile that spoke of the intimacies they'd shared long ago.

He wanted to ask her what she wanted, what she was trying to say. He wanted to growl his frustration with this vacation that was becoming too crowded. But he had too much of an audience, and before he could get to his feet and pull Sydney along with him out onto the veranda, Poe returned from the kitchen.

Her rummaging had produced a serving tray bearing eight highball glasses, a decanter of bourbon, another of water and a bucket of ice. Standing behind the chair she'd occupied earlier, she set the tray in the center of the table.

"Now," she said, continuing the conversation she'd dropped like a bomb. "Since none of us are sleeping together, let's get drunk and talk about sex."

2

"YOU HAVE GOT to be kidding." Lauren pulled her feet up onto her chair and wrapped her arms around her knees defensively.

"Not at all, sweetie. In fact, I'm dead serious." Poe tugged the stopper from the whiskey decanter and set it on the tray. And then she cast a wicked look around the table, teasing her dinner companions with a sinister gleam in her almond-shaped eyes.

Ever since Poe had made her observation of the room's sexual tension, Sydney had been waiting for the other shoe to drop. After all, she'd been warned earlier out on the veranda—a warning left wide-open, giving Poe plenty of leeway and absolutely no boundaries.

And so Sydney wasn't a bit surprised when Poe finally grinned and said, "Truth or dare."

Stunned silence greeted Poe's announcement. Sydney knew that, given another second, the gang would come around. But she wasn't going to wait that long. She was more than ready to get started, more than ready for fun. And, so, with a mental *Here goes nothing,* she reached for a glass. "I'm game."

Lauren gave an audible gasp. "You can't mean that."

"I can mean it. I do mean it." Sydney tossed ice

cubes into her glass and poured the bourbon. She looked down the length of the table, silently daring Lauren to say another word. "This is my vacation and I want to have fun."

"Truth or dare is fun?" Lauren asked, anyway, a brow raised.

"The right mood, the right company." Sydney lifted her shoulders, lifted her drink, glanced briefly at Ray as the fiery liquid slid over her tongue. The look in his eyes added to the burn, and it was all she could do to finish her reply. "Not to mention the right alcohol in the right quantity."

"I'll drink to that," Poe said, and finally everyone relaxed enough to laugh. Everyone, that is, but Lauren.

Lauren looked around the table, meeting one gaze after another, lingering the longest on Anton, whose expression was impossible to read. He definitely had stoicism down to an art, Sydney thought, but whether the look in his eyes was anger, intrigue or true indifference, she couldn't tell.

Lauren, obviously, wasn't having the same trouble. What she saw when she looked at Anton seemed to be all she needed to make up her mind. Decision made, she reached for the decanter and splashed a double over the ice cubes she'd added to her glass.

With a quick shake of her head, she downed a quarter of the drink, whistled, shuddered, then thumped the crystal against the table. "Fine. I'm in."

"All right," Doug said, and clapped his hands together. "I think we might just have ourselves a party."

At that, Anton grabbed his own glass and, not bothering with water or ice, downed the shot he poured. "Hell. If the subject is sex, count me in."

"Then sex it is." Poe pulled the stopper from the decanter of water and gave Sydney a quick wink. Sydney mentally crossed her fingers, hoping Poe hadn't gone too far. The last thing she wanted was for this game to backfire.

What she wanted, in fact, was for this game to rid the room of inhibitions. To rid Ray, in particular, of any hang-ups he might have that would prevent him from being open to her advances. Judging by the look in his eyes, however, judging by the way his gaze fairly simmered with uninhibited invitation, hang-ups weren't going to be a problem.

"So, Poe. Does your version of this game have rules? Or do we make it up as we go along?" Jess added two cubes of ice to two separate glasses, splashed both with bourbon and passed one to Kinsey. "I've got as good an imagination as the next guy but—"

"But like the next guy, you need direction. You just hate having to stop and ask." Smiling brightly, Kinsey toasted the other women with her drink and a round of high fives.

The men sat back, glowered and glared. Sydney had a feeling they were only biding their time. She'd yet to know a single man who didn't get a kick out of delivering a slam dunk comeuppance—especially to a woman.

"Hey, I asked. I asked." Jess tossed up his hands in exaggerated exasperation. "And like the next guy, I can't seem to get a straight answer, which is what I expected with a woman in charge."

This time it was the men exchanging the loud whooping endorsement of Jess's commentary on the female game plan. So, Poe did what any self-respecting woman would do when faced with a group of male chauvinists.

Leaning across the table, she beckoned him closer with the crook of one finger, running a fingertip over his lower lip when he met her halfway. "Why don't you put your money where your mouth is?"

Jess frowned, obviously confused by the switch in Poe's gears. "I don't get it."

"Since you seem to think I don't know what I'm doing, you figure out how this game should go down." She eased back into her chair. "Unlike you men, we women don't mind a bit when a man tells us what he wants us to do."

"I agree with Poe. Having a man in charge makes things run so much more smoothly." Kinsey scooted around in her chair and got comfy, having a whole lot of fun at Jess's expense as she stretched out her legs and crossed her ankles in his lap. "I just don't know what we'd do without you."

Jess ignored the batting of Kinsey's lashes, and smiling to herself, Sydney finally started to relax. Maybe a good time *was* about to be had by all. Poe's leap into the center of the tension was certainly proving a lot more effective than the eggshell route. Even Lauren had a grin on her face.

Jess rubbed his hands together, then he rubbed them from Kinsey's ankles to her knees. His brown eyes glittered and he lifted one dark brow. "Now this is more like it. Getting drunk, talking about sex, a man in charge and a woman in his lap. Doesn't get any better, does it, boys?''

His enthusiasm earned him a cuff to the back of the head from Kinsey. ''You're forgetting one thing, mister. And that is paybacks are hell.''

Jess thrust out his chin, tapped it with one finger. ''C'mon, then. Your best shot. Right here.''

Kinsey drew back a fist. Anton, sitting on her other side, caught her hand from behind. Sydney, in the chair next to Anton, leaned across and pried his fingers from Kinsey's, and when he turned to protest, she stuck out her tongue.

At the other end of the table, Lauren poured herself another drink. ''Enough, you people.'' She used her glass as a gavel. ''Let Jess explain his rules.''

''No kidding.'' Doug refilled his own glass, going for more water than whiskey. ''If I'm gonna get lucky tonight, I'm all for getting this show on the road.''

Poe lifted a brow. ''Weren't you the one talking earlier about taking matters into your own hands?''

Ray chuckled, shaking his head and reaching for his drink. He met Sydney's gaze over the rim of the glass he lifted to his mouth. His eyes were bright, a beautiful green, his gaze sharp and intent in both focus and connection.

Shivering, Sydney raised her glass. This was exactly what she wanted. This anticipation, this attraction. This slow, simmering arousal that was beginning to sweeten the stakes of the evening. She sipped her drink. The whiskey burned and she lifted her chin as she swallowed.

The motion drew Ray's attention. His eyes flashed and, as he lowered his glass to the table, he blew out a long, slow breath and briefly closed his eyes. Sydney blinked, but looked away as she lifted her lashes. As much as she wanted to hurry, she wanted to wait, to take her time and savor the seduction as much as she planned to savor plucking the forbidden fruit from the vine.

She turned her attention back to Jess, who'd dislodged Kinsey from his lap and gotten to his feet. He placed both hands flat on the table and glanced around, making eye contact with everyone. "Here's how we play. Whoever I choose to go first will pick someone of the opposite sex and ask that person a question. That person then decides whether he—or she—wants to answer truthfully or go for the dare."

"And we have to come up with the dares, too?" Lauren asked, and Jess nodded.

Anton, slumped back in his chair with arms crossed, looked as if he'd swallowed a nastier alcohol than was ever stocked in the liquor cabinet on Coconut Caye. "What if the person answers, but someone else at the table knows for a fact that they're telling a lie?"

Sydney took a deep breath and held it, waiting for Lauren to jump down his throat. But it didn't happen. Lauren only stared somberly at her drink. Her wounded expression tugged hard on Sydney's girlfriend heartstrings. Why did relationships have to be so damned difficult?

Anton's question appeared to leave Jess stumped. Then he smiled, his dimples and his eyes flashing in that bad-boy way he had of looking at the world. "Then that person calls them on it, and they have to take the dare, anyway."

"Ouch. That's cold," Doug said.

Poe reached over and patted his shoulder. "All in the name of good, honest fun."

"Hey." Grabbing Poe's hand where her fingers lightly gouged his muscles, Doug added, "I resent that remark."

"More like you resemble that remark," Ray corrected.

"Thanks for sticking by me, buddy." At Doug's grousing, Ray laughed.

"Yeah, dude. This is supposed to be a battle of the sexes." Jess dropped back into his chair. "Whose side are you on, anyway?"

Ray splashed another shot of bourbon into his glass. "Let's just say I'm doing all I can to keep my getting-lucky options open."

The other three men razzed him with loudly voiced hoots and hisses and snickering laughter. All Sydney could do was stare at the liquid in her glass, knowing the smile on her face was bound to give her away. She wasn't sure she wanted everyone at the table to know of her plans before she'd had a chance to share her intentions with Ray. Before she'd shown him exactly what a lucky guy he was and done so in a more intimate setting, without an audience.

Poe finally and effectively killed the locker-room atmosphere by drumming her hands on the table. "Yoo-hoo, Jess. I think we all understand your rules. Now are we going to play or what?"

Jess turned his attention to Poe. "Yes, we're going to play. And since you started this mess and put me in charge, I've decided you get to go first."

Shaking her head, Kinsey clucked her tongue in

disappointment. "Put a man in charge and he still needs a woman to get things started."

"I hate to break it to you, Kinsey," Doug said, sitting between Lauren and Poe and ignoring the threatening glares from both women. "But not only can we get things started without a woman, we can finish things off the same way."

Poe waved off his comeback. "Tell that to the centerfold sharing your special moment."

Every man in the room squirmed.

"Imagination and touch are more important than visual stimulation to a woman," Lauren added, directing a pointed glance at Doug. "Which is why we can start *and* finish with or without the help of a battery-operated boyfriend."

"Good ol' B.O.B." Kinsey sighed. "A fresh supply of batteries and he never lets a girl down."

Anton snorted and rolled his eyes before downing half his bourbon. Doug, on the other hand, stared at Kinsey in disbelief. "Are you telling me that you get off every time you, uh…take B.O.B. to bed?"

Kinsey only smiled sweetly, tossing back her long blond hair. "Why don't you ask me that when it's your turn to play?"

Doug shook his head and under his breath muttered, "Women. More trouble than they're worth."

Poe dug an elbow into his ribs to shut him up. "You can get back at Kinsey and all of womankind later, after I get through getting back at Jess."

Jess groaned and thumped his forehead on the edge of the table before looking up and grimacing at Poe.

Poe crossed her arms on the edge of the table and leaned forward, sparing a glance for Ray at her left,

Doug at her right, then Anton across the table, before she settled her sights on Jess. "Now, Jess. Since we're discussing sexy toys, my question is this. Have you ever done it with an inanimate object and, if so, with what?"

Jess's expression remained deadpan. "Such as?"

"Oh, I don't know. A blowup doll. An apple pie. That sort of thing."

"I think Poe has been watching a few too many movies," Kinsey said, and Ray snickered. Then Doug snickered. Sydney couldn't help herself and she snickered, too. Jess remained totally cool. She had to give him credit.

"Are you talking all the way back to puberty?" he asked, leaning over the table toward her. "Or during my recent sex sabbatical?"

Poe leaned even farther over the table, until her breasts threatened to spill out of her top. "I'm talking any time during your life, sweetie, though I'd really like to hear more about this sex sabbatical."

Jess leaned forward, too. "Well, then, sweetie. I take the dare."

Jess's refusal to answer brought him everything from howls to sympathetic groans to hysterical laughter, the latter from Lauren, who Sydney was beginning to think had had too much to drink.

Sitting back with a smugly satisfied smile, Poe laced her hands behind her head. "Since you dug yourself in deep with that one, I'll make it easy on you. You have to kiss one of your dinner companions. Girl or guy, it doesn't matter. The only caveat is that you have to look like you mean it."

"That's it? That's his dare?" Kinsey registered the

complaint and Sydney followed with "That sounds more like a reward."

"And a punishment for whoever he chooses," Lauren added.

Jess scooted back his chair and got to his feet. "Tsk-tsk, ladies. I realize this is going to be hard on those of you who don't get to experience my incredible expertise."

Anton brought his fist to his mouth and coughed to cover up his exclamation of "Bullshit."

"Yeah. What Anton said. You can just keep your tongue to yourself, mister," Kinsey said.

Jess ignored the outburst and circled the table, passing each woman once before stopping behind Kinsey on his second trip around. With both hands on the back of her chair, he leaned down and ran the tip of his tongue around the shell of her ear, blowing softly until she shuddered.

Sydney's own heart fluttered wildly, and one look at Lauren and Poe confirmed that neither of the other women remained unaffected. Even knowing Jess was all bark and no bite didn't stop any of them from wanting to feel the nip of his teeth. Though, mused Sydney, not half as much as she wanted to be nipped by Ray.

"Now," Jess said to Kinsey, breathing the words into her ear. "Don't be giving me grief about my tongue when you obviously don't have a clue what you're talking about." And with that, he continued his second trip around the table.

Sydney held her breath as he passed behind her, and she caught Ray staring as she slowly let it go. She wanted to know what he was thinking, what it meant when his pulse ticked at his temple, when his jaw seemed to grind. She wanted to know if he possibly wanted her, and how she was going to sit through the rest of the evening until she could find out for sure.

No one at the table said a word when Jess came to a stop behind Poe's chair. She still had her arms raised, her hands laced behind her head, and Jess settled his palms on her elbows. Her mouth quirked slightly, as if she'd never had a doubt she'd end up as his choice.

He ran his hands from her elbows down her triceps and back up to her forearms before pulling her to her feet, pushing her chair out of the way with his hip as he did. Then he turned her, wrapped her arms around his neck, settled his hands on her hipbones above the low-riding waistband of her pants and backed her into the table.

When he lowered his head, Sydney found herself once again holding her breath. Jess nuzzled his lips over Poe's jaw and chin before moving his mouth to her mouth. He was tender and gentle and soft with his approach.

He wasn't grinding his hips into hers and slipping his tongue into her mouth as Sydney was certain everyone was expecting him to do. No, he was taking things slow, the way a lover would take things slow, letting go of Poe's hips and moving his hands up her body to hold her face, finally opening his mouth enough to coax Poe to do the same.

It was unbelievable, the way Sydney's pulse raced, the way she found herself unable to pull in anything more than shallow breaths. She glanced at Lauren, then at Kinsey. Both women were equally transfixed. But this time Sydney could not bring herself to look at Ray, even though she hadn't a doubt he was looking at her. The sensation of being caught in his gaze like a fly in a spider's web was enough to keep her from glancing over. Or from looking again toward Jess and Poe.

The suggestion of intimacy stirred Sydney's hunger unbearably, and she breathed a huge sigh of relief when the couple broke the embrace. She even joined in the applause that followed and finally felt able to come up for air once Jess had taken his bow and made his way back to his seat.

"Well, now," Poe said, slightly out of breath as she settled back into her chair. "You almost convinced *me* that you meant it."

"Then I guess I won that round," Jess said, not entirely undisturbed himself.

"I don't know." Kinsey shook her head. "For some reason I feel like *I* won."

Her comment brought the laughter the room seemed to need. That, and the whiskey that was obviously beginning to take effect. Sydney had purposefully sipped slowly and made sure to water down what booze she was drinking.

And a good thing, too, since Jess turned to her and said, "Sydney?"

She looked up, feeling a rush of nervous trepidation. "Yes?"

"Truth or dare. Since you have had a bit of an icy reputation in the past—" Jess paused, letting the implication sink in "—I'm curious to know if you had an orgasm the first time you had sex."

Sydney didn't even blink. Could Jess have possibly asked anything she would've wanted to answer less, considering the present company, who could call her on any lie she might try to get away with? The present company who had brought her off repeatedly through the hours of that long, hot, summer night all those years ago?

And so she sat back, crossed her arms, looked Jess straight in the eye and told him and the rest of the room the truth. "Actually, Jess, yes. I did."

Anton snorted, obviously in disbelief. Doug sat slack-jawed. Jess stared from beneath two raised brows. The women were more vocal. Their responses ranged from "No way!" to "Go Sydney!" to "You lucky dog!"

And then the circle of reactions came back around to Anton and his skeptical suspicion. "Give her a dare, Jess. She's lying through her teeth."

Sydney turned a steely gaze on Anton. "What makes you think I'm lying?"

"It's hard to believe any woman would come her first time. Half the time even women who know what they're doing fake their orgasms." Anton flinched as a half-melted ice cube pelted him in the center of his chest. He glared across the length of the table just as Lauren threw another.

"If she's with the right man, a woman can have an orgasm every time. But since it's hard to find a man willing to take the time to learn what a woman needs, it's no wonder women end up faking." Lauren popped a third ice cube into her mouth, sucked it free of whiskey.

Anton upended his glass and drained the remainder

of his drink. "Let's not forget that some women seem to be able to come at the drop of a hat. Sorta makes a man wonder why she keeps him around when she can obviously do her own thing as long as she's got the batteries."

"Hey, dude. I don't know what you're complaining about." Jess glanced from one-half of the quarreling couple to the other and back. "Finding a woman uninhibited enough to come sure takes the pressure off."

"Exactly!" Lauren exclaimed, then turned to Jess. "Thank you, Jess. It's nice to know that a man can appreciate a woman's sexuality without feeling threatened by it."

Anton got to his feet and Sydney held her breath, waiting for what she knew would be an explosion. But Anton surprised her by calmly grabbing the decanter of bourbon from the center of the table and not saying another word. And then he left the room.

For several moments no one made a comment, as if talking behind Anton's back was as bad as talking in front of Lauren. Finally Poe split the difference with a mumbled, "Well, since I managed to so beautifully blow that, I think I'll console myself with a quick and painless death by drowning. Or at least a long walk along the beach."

"Oh, Poe. You didn't blow anything." Kinsey reached across the table and took hold of the other woman's hands. "If you're in the mood for company, I'd love to come along. My head could use the fresh air."

Poe got to her feet, her gaze lingering on Jess as she asked, "Anyone else care to join us in walking off dinner and drinks and the rest of the evening's disaster?''

"I'm going to take a shower." Lauren stood, stared at the table's surface as if getting her balance or her bearings, then headed for the circular staircase separating the dining area from the villa's main room.

Once Lauren was gone, Doug slapped his hands on the table, jarring the room from its pensive mood. "I'm all for a walk."

"Me, too," Jess said, taking Kinsey by the hand and dragging her off toward the villa's front entrance. He stopped halfway there, looked back and held out his other hand for Poe. "Doug, Ray? Sydney? Let's go."

Doug rose and headed for the group.

Sydney stayed seated and shook her head, running a finger around the rim of her near-empty glass. "You all go on. I'm going to finish cleaning the kitchen, then head for the shower once Lauren is through."

"Ray? You coming?" Kinsey asked as she followed the others across the room and out the front door.

Ray glanced from Sydney to the departing group and back again. His brows drew down over clearly indecisive eyes. His lips pressed together uncertainly. He stepped closer to Sydney's chair and stared down, reaching out to tuck a lock of hair behind her ear. "You want some help?"

Sydney rubbed her cheek against his lingering hand, then looked from her glass up to Ray and, smiling, said, "Help with the kitchen or with the shower?"

Ray's breath hitched and he stared down at her, his

expression having darkened, the tic in his jaw a hard echo of the pulse throbbing in the hollow of his throat. ''Don't give me a choice you don't want me to make.''

For a moment, just for a moment, Sydney closed her eyes. It would be so easy to say yes, to drag him into the shower off the first-floor bedroom suite that no one but her father ever used. But as much as she wanted him, she wanted to wait, to let the tension build, to keep their liaison a private affair.

And right now there were too many people waiting for him to join them on the beach. So what she did was get to her feet, reach across the table and gather up as many of the highball glasses as she could manage with two hands. Then she turned to face him.

''Truth or dare?'' she asked, and as she did, Ray's mouth quirked upward. ''Would you rather I accept your help when we're liable to be interrupted any minute, or would you rather wait until we have time alone?''

''The truth? I'd rather wait.'' He looked off toward the door as if even now he expected to be interrupted. Then he looked back at Sydney, his eyes flashing, his smile a silent promise of seduction he intended to keep. ''The dare? You find us the time.''

''I DON'T KNOW why I ever agreed to this trip.'' Lauren pummeled the pink, satin-cased pillow, then crossed her arms and hugged it close. ''I knew this was a mistake the minute I found out Anton was going to be here.''

''So why'd you come?'' Sitting on the corner of Lauren's bed and wearing nothing but a lemon-yellow silk chemise, Sydney rubbed lotion into her freshly shaved legs, intending to ferret out Lauren's feelings for Anton in a private one-on-one, since Poe's more dramatic efforts had sent the two lovers off in opposite directions.

Kinsey was actually the one bunking with Lauren, as Sydney had chosen to share a double room with Poe down the hall. The other two women hadn't yet returned from the moonlit stroll they'd taken along the beach with three of the four men.

Anton hadn't left the room he was sharing with Doug since taking the decanter of bourbon and calling it a night. Sydney doubted he was in any condition to put one foot in front of the other, moonlight or not.

Lauren's condition wasn't much better. Unable to sit still, she bounced this way and that, crossed her legs, then stretched them out and flexed her toes. Finally she tucked two pillows behind her, kept the one in front, leaned back against the headboard and collapsed.

Unfazed and possessing the patience of a saint, Sydney snapped the squirt cap of the lotion bottle and repeated her question. ''Why did you come if you thought it was a mistake?''

Lauren finally accepted that Sydney wasn't going away and heaved a huge sigh. ''I know he's been seeing Poe. And I knew she'd be here.''

''And you couldn't stand a week at the office without her so you decided to come along?'' Sydney asked wryly.

''Very funny.'' Lauren glared, then sulked. ''The truth is, I couldn't stand thinking of the two of them here together.''

"So do you plan to stalk any woman Anton goes out with? Or tag along on all his dates?" Sydney asked, having a hard time keeping a straight face.

Lauren massaged both temples, then rubbed the heels of her palms over her eyes. "I know, I know. I regretted moving in with him. Now I regret moving out. I don't want him dating anyone else, but I'm not sure how I feel about him. Or how he feels about me."

"Don't you think it's time to find out?" Sydney wrapped her fingers around one of Lauren's feet and playfully, teasingly squeezed. "Don't you think being here together gives the two of you the perfect opportunity to see where exactly you stand with each other?"

"It might." Lauren's expression conveyed her irritation as sarcastically as did her tone of voice. "Of course we'd have a better chance if certain other people weren't here stirring up trouble. I mean, c'mon. What was that business with the way Poe cleared off the table, anyway? Rubbing all over Anton and Doug. And truth or dare? Give me a break."

Sydney shrugged, walking a fine neutral line between her friendships with the two women. "I think she was trying to break the ice. You have to admit it worked. Too bad Macy wasn't here to take notes for gIRL gAMES."

Lauren blew out an inelegant snort. "What I want to know is where Poe gets off thinking it's her place to break the ice?"

"Why don't you ask her?" Poe said, walking uninvited and unexpected into Lauren's room and plopping on the end of the bed opposite Sydney. "I wasn't intentionally eavesdropping. I came back for my suit—'' she dangled the black bottoms to the top she'd been wearing all day ''—and to ask if either of you wanted to join us in the hot tub on the sundeck. But now that I'm here, I'm more than happy to clear any air that needs clearing.''

''All right.'' Lauren cocked her head to one side and considered the other woman and her offer. ''This isn't exactly a tropical reality show, Poe. We don't need a cruise director. We're all adults. We know how to get along and how to entertain ourselves, thank you very much.''

Poe shrugged carelessly. ''Maybe so. But it's obvious that certain tensions exist between some of us that will ruin this vacation for others if not dealt with.''

Lauren pulled up her knees and pressed them into the pillow she held tightly to her chest. ''You're talking about me and Anton.''

''That, yes.'' Poe inclined her head, lifting both brows in a visual challenge. ''And your feelings toward me.''

''What about my feelings toward you?''

''Obviously they are hardly charitable. And obviously they are rooted in the fact that Anton has taken me out a couple of times since the two of you broke up.''

''Well, then, what else is there to say?'' Lauren asked, clearly believing she held the upper hand.

Sydney glanced from Lauren to Poe, who easily yanked away Lauren's hold by replying, ''You mean, besides the fact that you can't have it both ways?''

Frowning, Lauren asked, "What are you talking about?"

"Either you want to be with Anton or you don't." Poe got to her feet, begin untying the knots holding her sarong pants in place. "You can't dangle your feelings like bait, hoping he'll bite. That's hardly fair to him. It's certainly not fair to me. But most of all, it's unfair to yourself."

"And how do you figure that?" Lauren asked, watching along with Sydney as Poe's pants and barely there bikini panties hit the floor.

Poe slipped one foot, then the other into the swimsuit bottoms and pulled them on. "Are you dating anyone else?"

"I've been seeing someone, yes," Lauren answered, then, avoiding Sydney's gaze, hurried to add, "It's not serious, though. We're just very close friends."

"Are you happy just being very close friends? Or do you miss being in a committed relationship?"

"I don't see how that's any of your business."

Poe snagged her pants from the floor, tossed them over one shoulder and crossed her arms beneath her breasts. Sydney suddenly knew that Poe was about to breathe the fire by which she'd earned her dragonlady reputation.

"C'mon, Lauren. If you want Anton, go for it. If you love him, fight for him. Fight *with* him, if you have to. Because I can tell you right now that he won't be unattached for long. He's intelligent and successful. He's kind and he's funny and he's sexy as hell.

"If you're sitting around waiting for him to come

crawling back on his knees, it's not going to happen."
And then Poe's voice softened. "But you know that,
don't you? You know exactly what he's worth. And
exactly what you're missing, now that you don't have
him in your life."

As Sydney watched, tears filled Lauren's eyes. She
reached for Lauren's foot, wrapped a comforting hand
around her ankle. But before Sydney could soothe her
friend with heartfelt words, Poe said, "Don't cry,
Lauren. Get tough. Get mean. Stand up to him. Stand
up for what you want from him. There are so few
men worth fighting for. And you've found one.

"Don't let him go, because if you do, I guarantee
he'll be snatched up before you can blink. And I can't
say that I won't be the first woman in line."

3

WRAPPING AN ARM around a beam supporting the second-floor balcony, Sydney stared out across the stretch of white beach and over the rippling water.

The moon was high and full, and the light thrown across the sea and the sand was easily bright enough to see by. The view was almost no different at midnight than it had been at sunset, except the sky was now a velvet cape of star-studded indigo and the Caribbean a darkly mysterious surface of sinuous, white-capped waves.

She couldn't sleep. She wasn't sure if it was being in a strange bed or being in strange company. This group would try the patience of the pope. At least Lauren and Poe seemed to be headed toward an understanding, if not a complete truce. And though Sydney had never before considered enlisting outside help in her initiative to get Lauren out of her funk, Poe's direct approach had certainly given Lauren food for thought. And given Sydney a lot to consider, as well.

She supposed it wasn't easy for Lauren to see Anton in the company of any woman with their relationship so newly ended. But there was something about Poe as the other woman that might even have given Sydney pause. Poe made no effort to suppress her sexuality. She made no apologies for her candor. And she had the potential to make for tough competition as a business adversary or as a rival for the attention of a man.

Lauren certainly had Sydney's sympathy. She wasn't sure how she'd react if Poe was to take a sudden interest in pursuing Ray while here on Coconut Caye. Sydney supposed that after she'd worked him out of her system and out of her fantasies, after they were all back in Houston, he'd be fair game. Poe would be welcome to go after him, if she had a mind to, and Sydney would have no reason to object.

So why did the picture of Poe, or any other woman, in the arms of Ray Coffey suddenly have Sydney's claws flexing?

It had to be the bourbon, she decided, frowning, even while recognizing the explanation of "too much alcohol" as not making a whole lot of sense. She'd barely sipped enough of her father's stock to get a buzz. Too much of a lightweight to overindulge, she'd wanted to stay sober. The alcohol she *had* consumed had only served to loosen her inhibitions, allowing her to seize the moment and boldly make a move on Ray.

The come-on she'd made once the room had cleared had been more than effective, judging by Ray's effort to steady his ragged inhalation of breath. Standing there beside the dining table and looking up into his eyes, Sydney had been struck by the suppressed passion she saw simmering there. Her own breathing had been rattled, her chest constricted, her throat so tight she'd found it impossible to speak in a level tone.

And that was totally unlike her, responding in an overtly physical fashion when attracted to a man. She'd always prided herself on being cool, being in control, which had, unfortunately, served to further her Ice Queen image, no matter that she was anything but cold.

For most of the evening, she'd watched Ray covertly, not wanting him to catch her staring or to sense any of what she had on her mind. While the others had been caught up in the flirtatious rules of the game, Ray had, for the most part, sat silently. He'd thrown in two or three smart remarks as guys, being guys, were prone to do.

But he'd been distracted, which Sydney could tell by the way he'd studied his plate, smiling at random comments, toying with his glass but never really doing much damage to his drink. He'd remained as sober as she had and then he'd left the villa with the others. She wondered if he'd had much to say while in the hot tub, or if his thoughts had been as consumed as hers by their parting conversation. He'd dared her to find time for them to be together. She couldn't think of anything she wanted to do more. This vacation was taking a promising turn.

As if on cosmic cue, footsteps to her left brought Sydney's head around to that side. The sight that greeted her brought her train of thought to a skidding halt, brought her body heat to the point of fever. She'd thought her breathing labored earlier this evening, but that struggle for calm was nothing compared to the way that now as she looked at Ray as he approached, desire stole the air from her lungs.

He was barefoot and bare-chested, wearing only a

pair of long denim shorts that hit the bend of his knees. His hands were shoved in the front pockets and dragged his waistband down his abdomen. The light the moon threw across the veranda cast his body in uneven shadows. The scar on his chest stood out like a long, white scimitar, curving over his breast-bone, cutting a slice through the dark whorls of hair.

Even from this distance, thirty feet, twenty, fifteen, ten, Sydney could smell his clean skin and just-washed hair. And now that he'd drawn closer, drawn close enough to touch, she could see the still-damp ends brushed back from his face. But his eyes told the tale of his wakeful state of mind. His thoughts were as unsettled as hers.

"Trouble sleeping?" he asked, reaching the beam closest to the one she held on to and, facing her, leaning his shoulder against the support.

"I always have trouble the first night away from home." Hands curled around either side of the beam, she gave a small shrug. "Strange noises. Though, in this case, the *lack* of noise may be the culprit."

"Yeah," Ray said, working to keep a straight face. "Hard to relax with all those waves breaking onshore. Not to mention the breeze blowing through the palm fronds. Pretty damn noisy, if you ask me."

The moon's gentle glow softened Sydney's view of Ray's left side, keeping his right half in shadow. His entire body, in fact, was a contrast of moonlit skin and blue denim and shiny clean hair, and a rich silhouette.

Which meant he was seeing her the same way.

Sydney took a step back into the full shade of the covered veranda. She wore nothing but her lemon-colored silk chemise, with nothing but thin spaghetti straps holding the low-cut, slip-style garment in place.

She was clothed, covered, but still she felt vulnerable, with her face scrubbed clean and her feet bare. She'd wanted to be at her seductive best when dealing privately with Ray. Not looking as if she was ready to crawl into bed....

Facing the villa's second story, the view of the tropical night at her back, she leaned her head against the support beam and smiled, tucking her laced hands behind her. "It's hard because I'm enjoying the peace and quiet. I feel like if I relax, I'll miss something grand. I'm always that way my first night here. I'll be better tomorrow."

"You'll be exhausted tomorrow."

"Me? Are you kidding?" She glanced at Ray, glanced back, then let her gaze roam. He was too gorgeous not to give in to the visual pleasure. "I run on adrenaline half the time, anyway. Relaxing is harder to get used to."

Ray pulled his hands from his pockets, crossed his arms over his chest, tucking his fingers into his armpits. His pectoral muscles bunched and flexed. Mouth awry, he gave an amused shake of his head. "You haven't changed much, have you. You never were the stop-and-smell-the-roses type, even in high school. Always so serious. All the time."

Sydney crinkled her nose, afraid he was right and that her personality had retained too much of the restrictive qualities she'd worked so hard to loosen, certain she'd never be the free spirit her mother had chided her to be. "I suppose I should do more to relax."

"You're right. You should." His smile was broad and compelling. "What good is a vacation if you're too wound up to have a good time?"

"Oh, I won't have a bit of trouble having a good time," she answered, even while wondering what Ray considered a good time and if he'd find her notion of one boring. Extreme cost analysis wasn't quite the same game as extreme Frisbee. Of course, this time, this vacation, she was thinking more along the lines of extreme sex. "I always enjoy myself when I set my mind to it."

He studied her for several long moments. She felt exposed under the intense scrutiny and couldn't help but be aware of her complete nudity under her chemise. Was Ray looking at the way the silk draped her body? Or was he looking deeper, searching beneath her reserve for the reasons she'd never learned, except for their one time together, to spontaneously let go?

She wasn't even sure she could put a name to the cause of her self-restraint. And her actions even on the night they'd made love hadn't been as spontaneous as they had been calculated. That was one thing she wasn't sure she should ever let him know.

Finally he said, "Why do you have to work so hard at having fun? Fun should be what happens when you're not working."

She understood where he was coming from, but still… "You don't think working can be fun?"

He shrugged one shoulder. "Satisfying, sure. Exciting, you bet. And, yeah, I enjoy what I do. Probably more than a lot of guys. But I wouldn't call it fun. Never fun."

Sydney turned first her head, then her entire body

to face him…and was immediately struck silent by both the heroic fire and heat of loss burning in his eyes.

Here she'd been casually flirting, waiting for Ray to offer to show her how to relax, to help her have a good time. She'd been thinking about the fulfilling nature of her own work. She hadn't been thinking at all about what it was he did for a living. About the suffering and devastation he had to encounter in his efforts to minimize disaster and save human life.

Funny how cosmetics and accessories suddenly seemed such a shallow pursuit. And at the same time, how gIRL-gEAR's new teen-mentoring program took on a new significance.

The effort was one of which Sydney was proud. Of which Ray *could* be proud. Of which even her flamboyantly unorthodox mother would *have* to be proud.

Still, Sydney felt compelled to reach out and offer a sympathetic shoulder, even though she had a feeling that Ray's needs, if any, would be less about a shoulder and more about a willing ear. Or even a friend, though she doubted he opened up more than rarely. She could almost see the words waiting to tumble free.

She gave him an encouraging smile. "I guess your line of work wouldn't be. Fun, that is. Though it has to be dozens of times more rewarding than running a fashion empire."

Ray avoided her efforts to draw him into the conversation about himself. "Would that make you an empress?"

"No," she said, determined to try again later. "Just your garden variety CEO."

His mouth quirked into a lopsided grin as he shook his head. "Nothing about you has ever been garden variety, Sydney Ford. I knew that the first time I laid eyes on you."

"When was the first time you saw me?" She knew precisely the first time she'd seen him.

"My senior year," he said, moving to brace both hands on the balcony railing and leaning forward. He looked out to sea as he spoke. "You would've been a junior. You came into the computer lab where we were working on the school paper. You were with Isabel Leighton. She was dropping off a disk with one of her infamous last-minute stories."

He leaned farther forward, his forearms supporting his body weight as he laced his hands together. "You stood just inside the doorway with your arms wrapped around a stack of books. You were wearing pin-striped dress pants and a lacy white blouse in a school where the girls who wore anything that covered their legs wore jeans. Nobody wore dress pants. But then I found out who you were and it all made sense. Pin-stripes and lace were exactly what the Ice Queen would wear."

He turned his head. His brows drew together in a thoughtful frown even as he smiled. "What I never could figure out was why you went to public school. No one understood why you weren't enrolled in some private, rich-girl academy."

"My mother," Sydney admitted, realizing that, though the resentment had faded, the ramifications of her mother's decision remained. Her school years hadn't been particularly happy, even though they'd proved to be a strong foundation from which she'd learned to stand up for herself, to concentrate on taking care of Sydney Ford.

"My mother didn't want me to get a big head, thinking I was better than anyone else because I had money." Sydney hugged herself. "I don't think she got it that I stood out more at public school, that I never quite fit in. Even the other kids who had money labeled me a snob."

"Because you had so much more."

She'd often wondered how different her life would've been without money. Even now, her falling-out with her father was a betrayal rooted in the financial choices he'd made. Still, it wasn't about money as much as it was about broken promises....

"Nolan made his first million before he was thirty, did you know that? And my mother wasn't exactly a pauper. She came from money, yes, but her abstract oil paintings struck a chord with collectors. Her gallery showings sold out every time. She never depended on my father for monetary support." Though, to Sydney's chagrin and, more so, to her heartache, things had apparently changed.

Ray nodded, as if digesting the information. "And you're following in the family footsteps. Making a lot of money and doing it your way. Not depending on anyone but yourself."

Sydney wasn't sure whether to frown or smile, but finally went with the latter. "I'm going to take that as a compliment, even though I'm not sure if that's how you meant it. Yes, I grew up with the advantages of wealth. I never had to worry about how I was going to pay for my education. And Nolan did seed gIRL-gEAR.

"But I wouldn't have gotten the money from any venture capitalist if I hadn't known what I was doing. Trust me. Nolan's not *that* altruistic." Or at least, she mused with more than a touch of resentment, he didn't used to be.

Ray glanced over, hair falling over his forehead. His expression conveyed an unwavering understanding. "You don't have to justify your family's wealth to me, Sydney."

She took a deep breath, blew it out slowly. Why did she let herself get so worked up over money? "Is that what I'm doing?"

He shrugged, then looked back out to sea. "Sure sounds like it to me."

She stuck out her tongue, anyway. "Then it's all your fault for reminding me of feeling like I had to justify it to everyone in high school."

"Everyone except Isabel Leighton."

Sydney took a deep breath. Ray couldn't have known of her latest connection to the one friend from school who'd kept her sane, who'd put so many things into perspective, who'd given her support and a shoulder when she'd needed both more than she'd needed food and water. It was just a coincidence that he'd brought up the one name that, considering recent circumstances, gave her heart a jolt.

"Izzy was the best," Sydney said, working to relax. "She's still the best and has done amazing things with her life. But as far as high school went, you're right. She couldn't have cared less where I came from. She was that way with all her friends. I had other friends, too. Good friends. Just not as many as Izzy had."

"And not as many as you might've had at private school," he stated, standing up to face her.

"True," Sydney admitted, knowing it wouldn't help her cause to leave Ray with the wrong impression about her own schooling preferences. And so she gave in to the smile tugging at her mouth. "But the private schools Nolan was interested in weren't coed. Even if I didn't date, I still enjoyed going to school with boys."

Obviously curious, Ray asked, "Why didn't you date?"

"You're asking *me* that question? You'd get a better answer from any of the boys I graduated with. I think you know what they thought of me." She definitely knew what they'd thought.

But knowing hadn't helped her understand why none of them had bothered to get to know her. She might've appeared aloof and she'd definitely been shy. But nothing about her was cold. Her Ice Queen reputation had been grossly exaggerated. As Ray had found out.

"Yeah, I know what they thought. But you gotta realize boys that age don't have the ability to tell the difference between frigid and shy. They'll look for any scapegoat if it'll save their own hot-shit reputation. You made a good one." He shook his head, returned his hands to his pockets. "It's not very hard to figure out."

Sydney mentally backtracked to the middle of his explanation and frowned. How had he known she was shy? She was sure she'd never told him. She wanted to ask him more, wanted to hear who he thought she was. Wanted to hear in his own words why he'd wanted her to share his vacation.

Wanted to begin to understand her own attraction to him so she could begin to work her way beyond the allure. He wasn't even close to being the compatible and civilized man she'd envisioned sharing her life with one day. Yet lust, she was discovering, defied logic and unanswered questions.

So she simply stared, wide-eyed and mute, as he moved closer, near enough that she could feel the heat from his large and half-bare body.

She could smell his deliciously masculine scent, clean and sweetly spiced. The bath soap stocked in the villa, made by a woman on the mainland, was a blend of natural ingredients, including native grasses and herbs.

Ray wore the fragrance well, and Sydney could only imagine the thrill of nuzzling her nose into his skin. She'd always been enchanted with the contrast of a man's soft skin over his hard muscles. And she knew without a doubt that Ray would feel the same as he had in the past, while still feeling like a man she'd never known.

He stepped directly in front of her then so that the shadow from the support beam fell across the center of his body. He lifted one hand and touched an index finger to her cheek, trailing his touch back toward her ear.

"Talk to me, Sydney Ford. Help me figure you out."

Sydney's heart pounded. "You know who I am."

"No." He shook his head. "I know the woman

you want me to know. But there's a whole lot more to you than what you've let me see.''

He was getting way too deep, when she wasn't here for deep. She was here for fun, not self-examination. ''You know I'm wealthy, you know I'm an Ice Queen. What else do you need to know?''

''I don't care about your money. I told you that.'' He tucked a lock of her hair behind her ear. ''And we both know nothing about you is cold.''

''Oh, I wouldn't be so sure,'' she said with a shiver, feeling the tips of her breasts draw tight.

Ray glanced down, ran his finger the length of her throat to her breasts, where he circled first one pebbled nipple, then the other. ''Trust me, Sydney. You're warm and you're welcoming in all the ways heat matters. I've been there, remember?''

How could she ever forget? She'd tried for eight years to match the ecstasy she'd felt with Ray. No man had come close to arousing her body so fiercely. She'd been starting to believe her own press, the rumors of her own frigidity.

But here was Ray, barely touching her, and she was heating to melting point. Why did she heat only for him? Why had she always heated for him? She hated the idea that he had a proprietary claim to her sexuality. She hated the thought of any man owning her that way.

Ignoring the fiery tip of his finger, she boldly lifted her chin. ''That's sex, Ray. That's not me.''

''Yeah, it's sex. But it's more than sex.'' He'd moved his trailing finger back up to the hollow of her throat. ''You have to be warm and welcoming as a woman to be as warm and welcoming as you are sexually.''

''But I'm not that way,'' she softly admitted before closing her eyes. ''Not always.''

''Good.'' He leaned forward, whispered directly into her ear. ''I like hearing that.''

His breath was warm, his body was warm. She wanted to absorb all she could of his heat and couldn't help but move her hands to his hips, where she hooked her fingers through his belt loops. ''Why would it matter to you? It's not like we're involved.''

''You don't think we're involved?'' The exasperation in his voice caused Sydney to open her eyes. ''Any time we're in the same room we're avoiding each other. Either that or working on getting as close as we possibly can. If we weren't involved, then your body wouldn't respond the way it does to my touch.''

The fingertip he'd had resting at the base of her throat he now touched to the center of her chest, right at her breastbone above the neckline of her chemise. Then he drew it down her belly, circling her navel before taking the fiery line of contact even lower, over the mound of her pubic bone to the knot of her clit—where he stopped, pressed and teased with a butterfly touch.

Sydney shuddered, flexed her fingers into fists and pulled at Ray's waistband, urging him closer. He continued his seduction, wedging his knee between her thighs, opening her to the brush of air that blew beneath the hem of her chemise. Tightly pinching a strip of the silk, he rubbed the material back and forth between her legs until she whimpered.

''Don't tell me you react like this with any man,''

he demanded, his voice gruff. "Don't tell me you let any man who wants to touch you this way."

No man had ever touched her this way except Ray. No man had ever drawn her to the edge of orgasm with such a simple touch. "I've never reacted this way with anyone but you. Never...never."

Ray growled, a low-rumbling sound that rolled up his throat. "So why aren't we doing this all the time? Why do you blow me off every time I get this close?"

He was close now and she wasn't moving. At least not moving away. She was moving the way she moved for him in her fantasies, in her memories. Memories that suddenly seemed incredibly out-of-date.

"Maybe I'm afraid that what we had wasn't real. That I made up everything about what you did to me. That it never happened. I'd hate to think that it never happened."

"Trust me, Sydney, it happened." He let go of her chemise. "But maybe I'd better refresh your memory."

He moved his hands around to her backside, kneaded the muscles there and pulled her close. She felt his arousal, the barest brush of a denim-covered swell against the fabric of her nightgown, against her belly beneath, against the core of her body that ached to take him inside.

She wanted to laugh. She'd thought her plans for seduction so simple. But nothing about her involvement with Ray Coffey was simple. It was complicated and intense and as disturbing as a young woman's memory of the first time she'd made love.

"Okay, I know it happened," she said. "I know it

was good. I just can't help but wonder why, with you, it was so different than it's ever been since."

"You don't think that has something to do with it being your first time?"

This time she did laugh. "No, Ray. I know about first times. I have a lot of girlfriends, remember? And we talk. About sex then and about sex now. What you and I did…" She hesitated. How smart was it really to admit to him how much of what she was feeling, how much of what she had felt?

They had both grown up. They had both changed. And he was wrong about their involvement. All they meant to each other was a piece of the past. At least that was all he meant to her, all she'd let him mean to her. She had a life now, she had a business and she couldn't afford his type of distraction. "What you and I did…"

"I want to know, Sydney." He bunched her chemise into his fists and worked his hands beneath. "Tell me why me. I knew dozens of guys who wanted you. You turned them all down. Why did you say yes to me?"

Had she ever said yes to him? Or had it been more a case of Ray being in the right place at the right time, Sydney reeling from the fight with her mother, her mother's ugly dare and demand?

Sounds filtered up from the first-floor veranda, drawing her attention. Her fingers slipped free from Ray's belt loops and she settled her palms against his bare waist. "Shh. Listen. Do you hear that?"

Ray stilled, as well, one hand on her back, one on her backside, his gaze locked intently with hers as together they listened to a couple making love on the veranda below. Quiet moans and whispered shushes and giggles that were quickly muffled. Quelled gasps cut off before timbres and tones of voices were recognized. Breathy moans and sharp cries smothered with openmouthed kisses.

Hearing the sounds, the voices, the unmistakable vocalization of passion, aroused Sydney unbearably, even while she felt a stirring discomfort at being an unwitting bystander to another couple's intimacy.

"Do you know you sounded like that?" Ray asked. "Breathy and out of control. I've thought about that a lot. About the way you sounded. Almost as often as I've relived your response. You were something, Sydney. And I want to learn all the ways you've changed."

"I just don't get this, Ray." This is what she was here to figure out, so she could let the obsession go, let Ray go and get on with her life. "Neither one of us has a reason to be as caught up in that one moment as we both appear to be. Doesn't that bother you?"

Ray remained silent for a moment, then made a sound of irritation. "Not in the way it seems to bother you. Yes, I think about it. Every time I see you, I think about it. It's a natural association."

She glanced away. She supposed he was right. Didn't she do exactly the same thing? So why did she feel more frustrated than ever?

Was it only because his hands were roaming her body? Because she finally had her hands on him? Or was it more, a frustration that this encounter wasn't following the lighthearted script she'd written?

The sounds from the veranda below were no longer hushed and subdued. The sounds were, in fact, noisy and frenzied and sexy, and suddenly Sydney was in no mood to eavesdrop. What she was in the mood for was pulling Ray close, exploring his body the way she'd been too young, too shy, too nervous to fully explore before.

But even more, what she was in the mood for was being held in his arms, being touched tenderly, being gently, lovingly seduced. And that wasn't what she was supposed to be in the mood for at all. She was supposed to be wanting a wild, hedonistic fling, and here she was thinking warm and fuzzy.

She dropped her forehead to rest on his chest, where the hair tickled her nose and his heart beat like a bass guitar playing rhythm and blues. The mood was all wrong for her seduction.

This wasn't the time alone that she'd wanted to have. They'd verbally revisited too much of the past, complicating an already complicated situation that she wanted to let go.

Leaving a tiny brush of her lips over Ray's breast-bone, she stepped away from his touch and out of his reach. His brows were dark slashes over eyes now glittering with arousal.

She mustered her resolve. "I think I want to go in to bed. I feel like a voyeur and I don't like it."

As she walked away, Ray called a soft warning to her back. "We're not done here, Sydney."

She paused. "For tonight, we are."

Casting a sultry glance over her shoulder, she met his gaze. Oh, how he made it hard to go. "But tomorrow's another day."

ONCE SYDNEY LEFT the room, Lauren waited less than five minutes before hopping off the bed and heading to the set of suites on the other side of the villa's second floor. She wasn't sure that what she was doing was smart, but it was what she had to do.

As much as she hated giving the other woman any credit, Poe was right. Lauren would never have another chance like the one offered over the next few days to discover exactly where she stood with Anton.

Neither one of them had any appointments to keep or errands to run or the excuse of work to keep them busy. This was the perfect time to settle their relationship once and for all.

And it obviously was still a relationship of sorts, or they wouldn't be so sensitive to each other, so moody, so emotional and defensive. Poe was right about that, too. Poe seemed to be right about a lot of things, Lauren found herself grudgingly forced to admit. A grudge she needed to let go of, based on misconceptions as it was. And she would. But not yet. Not when Poe's attraction to Anton remained a sore spot.

Her hand on Anton's doorknob, Lauren took a deep breath and turned it, truly surprised not to find the room locked up tight. She didn't know why she was nervous. She knew this man better than she'd ever known any man, and he knew her better than any man had ever known her.

It was that knowing that upped the stakes, the realization of how fragile this moment might become if she didn't step carefully, if she didn't choose the right words, if she didn't resist retaliation for the barbs she was sure he would throw. The fact that he'd taken himself off to bed with a bottle was proof enough of his hurt.

But he was not innocent in this lovers' game they played. She would own up to her failings. She would not take responsibility for the wrongs he had to acknowledge.

The door opened freely, quietly, into the room of the same neutral tropical pastels that defined the villa's color scheme. Anton wore the same shorts of khaki denim he'd had on at dinner, but now his torso was bare but for a dusting of light-blond hair. He lay on the bed farthest from the door, both pillows behind his head, as well as the one arm he'd crooked back.

His other hand held the decanter balanced on the flat of his abs. It was a little less than the half-full it had been when he'd taken it from the table. He hadn't had much to drink, after all, which, Lauren hoped, meant he was sober enough, receptive enough, to talk.

Though the door was already opened, she knocked. "Do you mind if I come in?"

He stared at her with eyes that were clear and sober. "If I say no, are you going to go away?"

For a moment she considered leaving, but it hit her that staying was actually the easiest course to take. She came into the room and closed the door behind her. "Actually, no. I don't think I want to go. At least not just yet."

He gave a careless shrug with one shoulder. "All right. Say what you have to say."

"And then get the hell out?" she asked.

He didn't say anything. He didn't have to. She knew from his face she'd guessed right. But knowing he didn't want her there actually goaded her to stay. He wasn't the only one with a hard head.

And since his hard head was a big part of their problem, this seemed the perfect time to soften him up. And didn't she know better than anyone how to soften him up?

She made her way to the other bed, Doug's bed, scooted into the center and sat, legs crossed, facing him. She wore a soft cotton, melon-colored tank top that was really the top to her pajamas. The bottoms were the same brushed cotton in a Winnie-the-Pooh print, the set a birthday gift from Macy and nothing like Lauren's usual nightwear.

She wondered if Anton even noticed. It had been a long time since he had seen her wearing anything in bed. She wondered, too—

"What are you still doing up?" Anton frowned. "I figured after that performance with Jess and Poe earlier, you would've been standing in line for the next dare, since the game was all about sex."

Lauren lifted a brow. Why did he have to have such a problem with her sexuality? She thought he'd have been thrilled with her assertive nature, but for some reason he'd always counted it a strike against her. "Actually, the party broke up after you left. Everyone but Sydney is in the hot tub on the sundeck."

"So why are you here, instead of there? You want to fuck or something?" He watched her reaction carefully, no doubt expecting shock.

Masking her pain was much more difficult. "I might. But I thought maybe we could talk first."

He pulled the stopper from the decanter, set it on the bedside table and reached for his glass. He did it all while keeping his gaze steadily focused on her face. "You want we should talk about fucking?"

This time Lauren had to bite her tongue. "Why don't we start with talking about feelings?"

"Sure. Why not." He tossed back the bourbon he'd poured, wiped his mouth with the back of the hand holding the empty glass. "I feel…like fucking."

Lauren blinked, blinked again, working to hold back her rising temper. Anger wouldn't get her anywhere and would only serve to give Anton the upper hand. She was determined to take Poe's advice, to go for it, to find out once and for all if this relationship had a chance to be saved.

And if she wanted to succeed, she had to hold both her temper and her tongue. "That's the liquor talking, not you. The Anton I know is kind and smart and honest."

She let that sink in a minute, though his blue eyes remained unreadable and she wasn't sure she'd reached him on the level she'd hoped. "You've been pretty quiet today. I thought that since we're going to be here for a week and a half and will probably be seeing a lot of each other, we should talk about being friends. Or at least about getting along as best we can for the rest of our vacation."

When he didn't say anything, when he only continued to unblinkingly stare, she battled the horrifying sting of tears. In panic, she reached for the tank top's hem. "But hey, if all you want is sex, we can do that, instead."

She'd lifted her top only enough to bare an inch or two of her belly when he said, "Lauren, stop."

She froze, waiting.

He sat up, swung his legs over the side of the mattress, moving the decanter of whiskey to the bedside table shared by the two beds. With his knees spread wide, his hands flat on the comforter on either side of his hips, Anton stared at the floor as if searching for words.

Slowly she smoothed the soft cotton of her top back into place. Sitting here, watching him struggle for what he wanted to say, waiting for him to find the composure he sought, her confusion and hurt melted away. Unshielded at last, her heart swelled to near bursting.

It was so simple, really. She loved him. She had always loved him. But if she had to let him go, she would. She'd come to understand herself much better during their recent time apart. And she knew she would rather remain friends than ever lose complete contact.

When he looked up, his eyes were turbulent. "I would love to sleep with you, Lauren. More than anything. But I know this isn't the time. And I apologize for being crass. I'm frustrated and I don't need to take it out on you.

"Things have been…rough. I haven't done well—" he gestured with one hand "—dealing with all this stuff going on between us. I never thought it would hit me as hard as it has. Or in the ways and the places."

Lauren hadn't known her heart could contain more emotion. She scrambled off the other bed and up onto Anton's, kneeling at his back and wrapping her arms around his chest. His skin was warm, his body so comfortingly solid. "We can always be friends. No matter what else happens, I'd like to think we will always be there for each other the way friends should be.''

She nuzzled his ear with her cheek, closing her eyes as she remembered his scent, his taste, the feel of his hands on her body, his body in her body. She didn't want to lose those memories, and another part of her longed to create more, new experiences to treasure, even if she had to share them with less intimacy than before.

He reached up with one hand and covered both of hers lying flat on his chest. ''I could use a friend right now. I can't stand my own company anymore. Spend the night with me, Lauren.''

Her heart lurched.

''Just to sleep,'' he added, as if fearing she'd turn him down otherwise.

Silly man.

''To sleep, perchance to dream?'' She felt him smile, felt the muscles in his cheek and jaw move, felt the brush of his day-old beard on her face.

''If I'm lucky, yes. With you in my arms, any dreams I have should be *damn* sweet.'' Anton pushed to his feet, turned and pulled down the comforter and the sheet. ''Hop in, Shakespeare.''

Lauren scrambled beneath, rolling onto her side as the mattress dipped beneath his weight. He switched off the bedside lamp and plunged the room into darkness, a darkness that eased as her eyes adjusted and the light from the full moon filtered in through the room's open window.

Anton pulled her close, spooning behind her, settling their bodies into the comfortably familiar position. Neither one of them spoke another word, as if the connection they needed could only be made through the intimacy of their heartbeats sharing the same rhythm, their muscles relaxing in trust, their breaths slowing and deepening.

A soothing blanket of peace stole over their bruised souls and the two friends slept.

And slowly they began to heal.

4

RAY MADE HIS WAY to the kitchen the next morning before the housekeeper, Auralie Duarte, arrived from the servants' quarters located in the center of the island. The arrangement afforded her and her husband, as well as Nolan's guests, privacy when the couple's service was needed on Coconut Caye.

Ray hadn't slept well and needed coffee, a lot of coffee, strong, and in a bad way. He wasn't sure that caffeine was going to be enough to get him over the funk of not getting the rest he needed or the funk of not getting what he needed from Sydney.

And he wasn't talking about sex.

If getting her into bed had been his primary goal when he'd stepped out onto the balcony last night, he didn't have a doubt that he'd be even more sleep-deprived this morning than he was. He'd also be a helluva lot more relaxed—but then hindsight *was* twenty-twenty.

Having found the supply of fresh coffee beans and the grinder, he went in search of the coffeemaker Auralie hadn't yet pulled from storage. He found it in the back of a lower cabinet, pulled it out and cleaned the thermal carafe.

He hated grinding the beans, certain the noise would wake the four sleeping beauties sprawled across the sectional sofa in the villa's main room. But a man had to do what a man had to do, and he poured the beans into the grinder's chute.

With no walls dividing the structure's first floor, he supposed Doug and Jess, Kinsey and Poe were asking to be disturbed by falling asleep here, instead of upstairs in their respective bedrooms. He'd been the first last night to leave the hot tub; the others had obviously stayed and partied, though at least half of the party had moved from the deck on the roof of the villa to the veranda wrapped around the structure's first floor.

He still wondered who it was he and Sydney had heard beneath the balcony last night. Hell, for all he knew, it could've been Anton and Lauren making up for several months' worth of lost time. But still, the sounds had stayed with him and kept him awake. Kept him thinking of Sydney and their one incredible night together.

At that time and at that age, he'd never talked to another woman the way he had to Sydney, never made love to another woman as many times in one night, never held another woman while she'd cried over the breakup of her family. Never felt as helpless, either. He hadn't known what to say or what to ask.

Ray admitted he hadn't done much better last night. He had years of experience pulling people from burning buildings, digging survivors from beneath tons of rubble, cutting through twisted metal to reach victims of accidents.

But none of those challenges matched the delicate job of probing Sydney's mind and heart.

Back in the States, in full CEO mode, she had shut

him out and shut him down every time. And now she'd taken things so far in the other direction that he was at a loss. Maybe her seven-year itch was back. The boy he'd been had always had a big head at being the chosen one, even while wondering why him and why now? The man he'd become was equally curious. But this time he'd get some answers.

Ray hit the grinder's switch. The aroma of rich Jamaican Blue Mountain filled the kitchen air. The blades whirred and he kept an eye on the main room, watching as first Poe, then Kinsey began to stir. Jess and Doug followed, or at least managed to open their eyes. Neither one of them made an effort to get to their feet, instead sitting and watching the women stumble and stretch.

Maybe, Ray thought, he needed to take another tack. Maybe he'd take the pressure off Sydney and he'd be the one to find time for them to be alone together. Then he'd make sure he was tuned into her frequency.

The grinder's blades finished the job with a sudden high-pitched whir. Ray shut off the motor and measured the freshly ground beans into the filter basket. While he filled the reservoir with water, Poe came into the kitchen and found five mugs. She lined them up on the countertop.

"For coffee, I'll forgive the intrusion into my dreams. Ray, you are definitely a man after my own heart." Wearing the fire-engine-red terry cover-up she'd zipped over her bikini last night, Poe hopped up onto the counter and waited for the coffee to brew.

"Hey, dude," Jess called from where he still sat sprawled on the sectional, his jaw dark, the circles under his eyes even darker. "You still planning to hit the Jet Skis with us this morning?"

Ray had no idea when Sydney would make it downstairs. But it didn't really matter. Privacy wasn't going to happen anytime soon. He might as well pretend he was here on Coconut Caye for a vacation.

"You betcha," he said, and wrapped his hand around the nearest mug and waited for the coffee to brew.

ANKLES CROSSED, Sydney sank onto the beach towel she'd spread out on the pier that jutted away from the front of the villa and into the sea. Lauren sat beside her, squinting at the rest of the group tearing up the waves on Jet Skis. Sydney handed Lauren the sunglasses she'd left on the kitchen counter.

"Thanks." Sliding the Oakleys into place, Lauren adjusted the left strap of her Brazilian-cut bikini, turquoise with big fuchsia circles. "That's better. This morning I'd probably have forgotten my head if it wasn't attached to my shoulders."

"That bad a night, huh?" Sydney was dying to ask more, especially to find out exactly where Lauren had spent the hours between midnight and two, but figured it was best to let her friend spill her guts at her own pace.

"Actually, I slept like a log." Lauren stretched her arms overhead and yawned.

Uh-huh, Sydney thought, wondering why, if Lauren had slept so soundly, she was yawning as if she hadn't slept a wink. "You weren't out on the downstairs veranda around midnight, by any chance, were you?"

"No. Why?"

"I thought it might've been you I heard moving around down there."

"Wasn't me. Anton and I talked for a while, then, believe it or not, we went to bed and to sleep. No funny business or fooling around or anything." Lauren shook her head in disbelief. "I can count on my fingers the number of times we've gone to bed at the same time and done nothing but sleep."

"Really? Wow. Let's think about that. You were together about four hundred days, give or take." Sydney could hardly keep a straight face. "That's an awful lot of condoms, girlfriend."

"Ha-ha-ha." Lauren screwed up her face. "You know what I mean. We didn't always go to bed at the same time. But if we did—"

"Then you got lucky," Sydney finished, listening to the motors of the watercraft rev and catching the unmistakable whiff of burning fuel.

"Actually," Lauren amended, tilting her head to one side as she considered her reply, "I like to think of it as Anton getting lucky. That way it's easier to convince myself that he's miserable without me."

"Instead of you being miserable without him?" Sydney asked, knowing the question was totally redundant.

"It shows, doesn't it?" When Sydney nodded, Lauren buried her face in her hands, then shuddered away her self-pity and looked up. "It's not a case of simply being lonely. I know that. I haven't exactly been sitting at home feeling sorry for myself all this time."

"So I've noticed." Sydney had so wanted to talk

to Lauren about whatever was going on between her and Nolan and could've kissed her friend for the opening.

Lauren grimaced. "I love your father to death, Sydney. But as wonderful a man as he is, he's never been more than a friend."

Relief washed over Sydney like a breath of fresh air she hadn't realized she desperately needed to breathe. "That's good to know. Because as much as I adore you, and I do adore you, you know that…" She refused to go on until Lauren nodded. "Good. Because, as much as I adore you, you are not the woman my father needs in his life."

Sydney waited, thinking Lauren might object or complain that she'd been insulted. Instead, Lauren seemed to need time to think. She sat with her mouth pressed in a tight line, returning Poe's wave from where the other woman had slowed her Jet Ski in front of Anton and Ray.

"Want to know something?" Lauren finally asked, glancing at Sydney. "Your father needs someone like Poe."

"Poe?" Annabel Lee and her father? Sydney was totally taken aback. "You've got to be kidding."

"Nope." Lauren shook her head. "You see your father as a father, Sydney. Trust me. I don't see him as a father at all, if you want to get down and dirty about it. And I really could see him and Poe hitting it off. She's older, well, older than we are, anyway, by, what? Five years, I guess? Anyway, she has a really unique sophistication that I think would fit with your father's way of life."

Sydney couldn't disagree with Lauren's assessment

of Poe's attitude and outlook, especially with all she'd recently learned while considering Poe's promotion. But she wasn't going to admit that Poe, as a woman, would make a good partner for Nolan Ford.

"I don't know. I can't see her chasing my father on a Jet Ski. Or challenging him to a game of truth or dare."

"Maybe that's because you don't want to see it," Lauren observed wisely.

"Now, that is a very real possibility." Time to change the subject. "The only possibility even more real is the one where I want to see you and Anton back together."

Lauren sighed, shrugged, sighed again, as if whatever was going to happen was beyond her control. "We have a lot more talking to do. Last night he was angry…at himself, I think, more than at me. Neither one of us said everything that needs to be said, but he held me. And that said a lot."

Sydney couldn't think of anything more to add. She stared out at the water and especially at the two men now straddling their surfboards. The surf had long since died.

Much as she sat talking with Lauren, Anton sat talking with Ray, legs dangling in the water, hands gripping the edges of the boards. Both men wore sunglasses secured with a rubber lanyard and knee-length board shorts. Their shoulders and their backs both gleamed with a healthy tan, perspiration and sunscreen.

The air, in fact, carried the distinct aroma of coconut oil, in addition to the wonderfully salty scent of the sea. Sydney took a deep breath, braced her hands on the pier behind her and leaned back, enjoying the breathtaking view of the waves and the spectacular scenery Ray Coffey offered.

He'd already left the kitchen by the time she'd finally made it downstairs this morning. In fact, Lauren and Auralie had been the only two still around. After a quick cup of coffee, Sydney and Lauren had let Auralie shoo them out of the kitchen. The efficient, sturdily built woman had refused to let them help prepare the rest of the day's meals.

Sydney had headed back to the bedroom she shared with Poe, showered and decided on a copper-colored maillot. The suit plunged low in the front, even lower in the back and was certain to snag Ray's attention. After last night, she refused to be caught looking any way but her best.

She also refused to let Ray draw her into a deep exploration of their shared past. They both knew it existed. They both knew they remained connected because of that one long-ago night. But Sydney did *not* want to revisit the rhyme or the reason for the things they'd done.

She wanted to revisit the passion, if it existed anywhere but her memory, and burn it out of her system once and for all, so she could let the entire episode go. She had to let it go. She had to maintain her professional focus, had to separate business from pleasure. If not, she'd fail in the first and ultimately lose out on the second.

And even worse, she'd have learned absolutely nothing from the mistakes of her mother and father.

"So what's going on with you and Ray?" Lauren asked, breaking into Sydney's thoughts.

She cast a glance over the rims of her sunglasses at her friend. "What about Ray?"

"Not Ray. *You* and Ray." Lauren returned Sydney's over-the-rims-of-her-sunglasses glare. "He totally avoided looking at you during your truth-or-dare answer. Like, as soon as Jess asked the question, Ray couldn't study his plate hard enough."

Pushing her sunglasses back into place, Sydney gave a shrug. "Who knows? Maybe the idea of female orgasms makes him nervous."

Lauren laughed. "Ray Coffey? The man who rushes into collapsed tunnels and burning buildings for a living? Nervous about *anything?* Try again."

"Sure, he's a big tough guy. That doesn't mean he's comfortable talking about sex." Sydney really did not want to go here, and had a feeling she wasn't pulling the wool over Lauren's eyes, anyway.

"Uh-huh, right. He barely flinched when Jess kissed Poe, but the minute the conversation turned to your sexual experience, he was squirming like he was the one in the hot seat." Lauren swiveled around on her towel so that she was facing Sydney. The sun glinted off the dark surface of her glasses. "Why would Ray feel like he was the one in the hot seat, Sydney?"

Well, hell, Sydney mused. Why shouldn't she share what she was thinking? She'd definitely be interested in Lauren's reaction. As a friend and as a woman with a different perspective on Ray. "The truth? I was thinking of having a vacation fling."

"With Ray Coffey?"

"No, with Anton." Sydney rolled her eyes. "Of course, with Ray. Who are we talking about, silly?"

"Hmm," was all that Lauren said.

Sydney huffed. "What is that supposed to mean?

Lauren shrugged, then turned back to face the wild bunch cutting up the waves. "I guess I can see you and Ray having a fling. He's definitely a hunk. Perfect fling material."

"True," Sydney said. "Even though you have to admit he's more than a hunk."

For a moment Lauren didn't reply. Then softly and slyly she said, "You don't need a man to be anything more than a hunk if you're only going to have a fling."

When put that way, Sydney didn't like the way her plan sounded, which was cheap and sleazy, when what she'd envisioned was definitely hot and sexy. She hated to ask, because the possibility was so far-fetched. Still, she was curious.

Casually she turned toward Lauren. "What if it turns out to be more than a fling?"

"Why? Are you thinking long-term? With Ray?" Lauren leaned back on her elbows and lifted her chin to the sun. "I could've seen you with Leo Redding. A corporate attorney is more your type. I'm not sure I can see you with Ray."

Lauren's added comments made Sydney sound as if she cared what Ray did for a living. She was in awe of what he did for a living. "I think Ray's profession is totally noble and honorable. Did you know he spent time in New York last year?"

"Give me some credit, Sydney. I don't think what Leo does makes him any better than Ray. I just don't see Ray putting up with the fund-raisers for long. He's way too physical." Lauren shook back her hair;

the ends dragged over her beach towel. "He could hardly sit still at the Wild Winter Woman fashion show last month."

True, Sydney thought, watching as Ray paddled his surfboard out toward Doug's Jet Ski, both managing to trade places without dumping either men or machines into the sea. "Physical" was definitely an adjective that described Ray Coffey. Both in his appearance—his body was amazingly fit and firm—and in the way he moved. Sydney so enjoyed watching the way he moved.

"By the way," Lauren said, cutting into Sydney's musings, "I did notice *after* the fashion show that he and your father certainly were chummy. You have any idea what's going on with them?"

Sydney lifted one shoulder in a perfunctory shrug. "My first guess would have to be money. With Nolan, it's usually about money."

"You think he'd try to buy Ray somehow?"

"No way," she said, shaking her head sharply. "Nothing like that. I was thinking more along the lines of a donation. Especially in light of all the funds raised for firefighters this past year."

"Oh." Lauren squirreled around to lie flat on her belly while still facing the sea. "I thought maybe he was buying him for you."

"For me?" The thought had never even crossed Sydney's mind. "Why would Nolan buy a man, buy Ray, for me?"

"I don't know. To make sure he gets the son-in-law he wants, I guess. But I doubt that's the case. It doesn't seem Nolan's style, even though I don't know him the way you do."

"Son-in-law? Like I have time in my life for dating, much less for a husband?" Sydney shook back her hair. "Right now, I barely have time to take a vacation. And I wouldn't be here if I didn't have faith in Macy, Chloe and Melanie not to let things at gIRL-gEAR go to hell."

And that was the thing. Until this past year, Sydney would've agreed with Lauren about what was and wasn't Nolan's style. But during the past twelve months, Sydney's father had done a lot of things with his money she never would've expected, as well as not doing the things he'd promised to do.

But *buying* Ray Coffey? Sydney found a transaction of that nature hard to believe of either man. Even harder to believe, however, was the irony of the entire suggestion.

Her father possibly buying her the very man to whom she'd lost her virginity? Not to mention the fact that she'd done so in the heat of anger at her mother's daring her to "get the stick out of your ass, have some fun and, for God's sake, get laid?"

Inevitably, inexorably, Sydney's gaze moved back to Ray. How would an honorable and noble man react after learning he was a convenient body at the right place and the right time? Despite the tropical heat, she shivered. That was one skeleton best left in her closet.

This conversation wasn't headed in any direction Sydney wanted to go. Why couldn't she have her fling and enjoy it, without having to take trip after trip down memory lane?

She got to her feet and handed Lauren her head-hugging metallic sunshades. "Hang on to these, will you? I'm going to have a swim."

"I'll put them in here with mine," Lauren said, tucking both pairs down into her woven carryall. "I think I'll join you and see if I can talk Anton into some underwater hanky-panky."

Sydney stared at the other woman. "I thought you and Anton still had a lot to talk about."

"We do." Lauren stood and made quick work of putting her long hair into a single braid and securing it with a scrunchie. "But I can talk with my hands as well as I can with my mouth. And I don't need words to do any of it."

"You're impossible," Sydney said, more than a bit jealous as she watched Lauren execute a shallow dive off the pier. Sydney followed, welcoming the refreshing feel of the water.

Coming up for air, she shook drops of salty spray from her face, wishing it was as easy for her to "damn the torpedoes—full speed ahead" as it seemed to be for Lauren. But it wasn't. And it probably never would be. Which meant a vacation fling was just not her style.

But Sydney Ford worked in fashion. And as anyone who had anything to do with the industry knew, styles changed.

BY THE TIME the dinner hour rolled around, the vacationers were exhausted. A day spent in the sun and the surf guaranteed that none of them had the strength or the energy to do more than sprawl across the braided rug covering the main room's floor or across the sectional sofa.

Having spent less time than the others battling the waves and the powerful Jet Skis, Sydney and Lauren, both freshly showered and smelling like herbal soap and coconut shampoo, headed to the kitchen to help Auralie prepare a light meal of salad and roast-chicken sandwiches.

Ray's stomach was rumbling. He was absolutely starved. But he was also totally beat and knew that a heavy meal would put him out. He wanted to stay awake as long as he could. He wanted Sydney to finish up in the kitchen, bring the sandwiches as she'd promised and sit in his lap while he ate.

If she wanted to feed him while she was there, he wouldn't object. He wouldn't turn down a woman's offer of personal service. Like most guys, he enjoyed and could get used to being waited on. But all he really wanted was to have her close.

Funny how his needs had grown simpler over the years and how he'd learned that a woman's companionship, even her quiet presence in the same room, brought a pleasure all its own. Funnier still, how he'd never put Sydney into that category until now, watching her with Lauren in the kitchen.

Sydney had a touch of sunburn on her nose and had pulled the layers of her shoulder-skimming blond hair into a careless ponytail. She'd changed out of that metallic-looking swimsuit that showed off her body in ways her bikini had never managed and now wore a plain yellow T-shirt and a pair of plaid pastel walking shorts.

She was laughing with Lauren as they worked, totally at home in the kitchen and looking nothing like gIRL-gEAR's CEO. Instead of her usual one-hundred-percent immersion in business, she was having one-hundred-percent pure fun. She wore minimal makeup, only enough to highlight her bright blue eyes and accentuate a complexion that Ray knew had the feel of the smoothest silk.

Great. Now he was waxing poetic about a woman's eyes and skin. Yep, big tough guy, all right, he groused, pulling his gaze from the kitchen and back to the movie. After rifling through the extensive collection of DVDs stored in the main room's bamboo étagère, Jess had grabbed two of the sectional's throw pillows and made himself at home on the floor.

Ray and Anton sat at opposite ends of the sofa, and Doug had commandeered the one and only recliner. He now sat feet up with his head back, half-asleep while the twenty-five-inch screen played Tom Hanks's *Apollo 13*. Poe sat in the center of the sofa putting tiny braids into Kinsey's hair while Kinsey sat cross-legged on the floor.

The scene was almost surreal and resembled nothing from any vacation Ray had taken before. Of course, it had been years since he'd enjoyed a real vacation. The last one had been a bust, a total disaster from which he'd never recovered, taken three years ago with two of his fraternity buddies and his only brother, Patrick.

Having completed his master's thesis while working as a firefighter in College Station, Texas, Ray had been ready to let loose. The four men had flown out of Houston and into Barbados, ready to party their backsides off with tropical drinks and tropical women. Hot days and hotter nights and late, lazy mornings spent sleeping off the deadly combination of sex and rum. Paradise and heaven rolled up in a big fat cigar.

What none of them had counted on was the reality of the myth of modern-day Caribbean pirates. Drug runners with no care for property and even less for human life. Buccaneers in golf shirts and cargo shorts, baseball caps and deck shoes, automatic weapons slung across their backs.

Ray shifted on the sofa, glanced across the room toward the kitchen and Sydney, then back to the movie, which was nothing but a big blur. Suddenly he couldn't sit still and wait for Sydney, sandwiches or not. He pushed off the sectional and headed for the circular staircase that led to the sundeck on the villa's roof.

The evening breeze, which hit him full in the face, was welcome. He shook off his stale musings and drew a deck chair close to the waist-high safety railing, propped his feet on top and, through slats that reminded him of prison bars, stared out across the tops of the coconut palms toward the sea.

He hated thinking of his brother. Patrick was never far from his mind, but he'd learned to keep his thoughts put away. He'd also learned not to let random events shoot the lock he kept on that particular emotional trigger. Even now he didn't know why, except for the vacation comparison, he'd let his thoughts drift to Patrick.

Ray really did know better. What had happened three years ago wasn't his fault, wasn't anyone's fault. But the guilt remained. And guilt was something he couldn't have hanging over his head. Not if he expected to do his job with any level of competence and detachment.

Right now, the last thing he felt was detached. Not from his memories of Patrick, the brother he'd sworn to protect, the brother who would've turned twenty-five last month if he'd been around to have a birthday.

And not from Sydney Ford.

He was supposed to be here on vacation, and she was supposed to be his good-time girl. She'd grown up in a big way, while he hadn't been around to keep track. And his good-time plans were now X-rated and very, very adult.

The thought of Sydney, the woman, naked beneath him or, better yet, naked on top, where he could watch her body move and see the expressions she couldn't keep from her face, had him squirming in the cedar deck chair. He couldn't imagine how he'd be squirming when he had her there above him, holding her hips while she rode him.

As if he'd conjured her up, she appeared, her bare feet slapping lightly on the boards of the deck. Handing him a plate with two huge sandwiches, she set a bottle of water down by his chair before she leaned back against the railing and dusted her hands together.

He grinned his thanks.

"Don't get used to the personal service," she said as he bit into the homemade bread and tender chunks of chicken. Her mouth twisted with amusement when she added, "And that's all I have to say about that."

The personal service he wanted from her had nothing to do with food. It was a good thing he had his mouth full, because he might have said so.

"You're not in the mood for Tom Hanks?" she asked, glancing up at the gorgeous night sky.

He looked at her long neck, at the curve of her throat, her smile, the fullness of her breasts. He swallowed—first his sandwich, then a hard knot of desire. Finally he shook his head. "Sorry, no. And if you're in the mood for company, I'm not sure I'm your best choice."

Looking at him, she cocked her head to one side and drew her brows into a thoughtful V. "Why the bad mood?"

What exactly was he supposed to tell her but the truth? he thought, then took a deep breath, blew it out. "I didn't know it would be so rough coming here."

She frowned. "Why would it be rough coming here?"

He'd taken another bite and had his mouth full of sandwich. It made for a good excuse not to have to talk until he'd figured out exactly what he wanted to say, what he wanted to tell her, what he wanted her to know.

Her hands braced on the deck railing, Sydney went on, "Are you sorry you brought all of us with you? Or is it about the *Indiscreet*? I hate that you didn't get to finish the cruise you were promised. Nolan's been looking to sell the boat for a while. I guess it's a good thing."

Ray took a slug of water from the bottle to clear his throat and down the rest of his sandwich. "Don't worry about the boat. It's not that at all. And I'm glad everyone's here. I'm especially glad you're here."

"Then why are you hiding on the deck?"

"I've been thinking about Patrick," he answered before second thoughts had a chance to stop him.

"Oh, Ray." Sydney closed her eyes, rubbed a hand over her forehead as if wondering how best to ease his pain. Then she swiftly looked back up. "I'm so sorry. I haven't thought about Patrick in so long. I never knew exactly what happened. I knew he'd disappeared, but have you never heard a word?"

He really didn't want to get into Patrick's disappearance with Sydney. At least not now, not when it weighed so heavily on his mind, not when he was really more interested in using her body in ways that would keep him from thinking about anything at all.

But he knew he needed to talk. Until now, he'd never wanted to. Until now, he hadn't had Sydney to listen. "Patrick and I and two of my frat brothers had gone to Barbados. We were celebrating—or at least *I* was celebrating—finishing my master's."

Sydney's eyes widened. "Wow. I didn't know you'd done your master's."

He nodded, gave a half-hearted shrug of one shoulder. His degree hardly seemed to matter anymore. "I didn't have much of a life from eighteen to twenty-four, if you want to know the truth. What life I did have was all books and study and a lot of brushfires gone out of control."

"How did you manage grad school and fighting fires? Didn't you ever sleep?"

"Sure." It seemed so long ago now that it probably had been a bigger deal than he was making it out to be. "But long shifts at the firehouse make for perfect study time. And most of my professors were big believers in the Internet. I attended more than a few lectures via videocam.''

''I feel like such a slug.'' Pushing her bangs from her forehead, Sydney ran both hands back over her ponytail. ''I've thought more than once that I need to find the time or make the time to go back. Chloe's going back this fall, did you know that?''

Ray shook his head. He didn't keep tabs on any of the gIRL-gEAR partners except for the one who held his interest. ''It's a good thing. A feeling of having accomplished something. Having stuck it out, which sometimes I think is all a degree really means.''

''Better than the feeling of accomplishment you get from your work?'' she asked, her hands moving back to the railing.

''Not really.'' He wasn't sure he could explain. ''Just different. I like to feel I'm doing something positive with my time and my life. Work gives me that. School did, too.'' He wasn't sure he could clear it up enough for her to understand. ''It's a lot better than feeling like I've failed.''

''Is that how you feel about Patrick? That you let him down somehow?''

''I didn't just let him down.'' Ray looked away from Sydney and off to the side, where the moon shone on the tops of the coconut palms. ''I failed him a hundred ways to Sunday, plain and simple.''

''I don't believe it's that simple for a minute,'' she said, shaking her head. ''I don't know you as well as the best of your friends, but I do know you would've done whatever you could do to find him.''

She couldn't know. No one knew. No one had any idea of the dead ends he'd hit, the leads he'd exhausted. "I've spent so much time looking. So much time. And nothing. Not a single clue. It's like he vanished off the face of the earth."

"What happened?" she asked softly.

He felt the rush of words before he could figure out how to stop them. "We'd rented a sailboat and were making our way through the Virgin Islands. We had a guide, the boat owner. We weren't totally stupid. We'd planned to do a lot of drinking and needed someone to keep us from taking ourselves out across the Atlantic. Besides, he promised us he knew all the best places to find warm, willing women."

Sydney crossed her arms and shook her head with mock disdain. "Booze and women. I suppose boys will always be boys."

He liked the way she sounded all high and mighty, because he knew she was nothing of the sort. "We drank and screwed our fair share, to tell you the truth. Patrick thought he'd died and gone to heaven."

"What happened?" Sydney prompted again. "If you don't want to talk about it, I understand. But I'd really like to know."

"We were boarded by pirates."

"What?" she gasped.

"Unbelievable, right? But it's true. Another boat. They waved us over. We thought they were in trouble. They were signaling that they had no radio. And there was some serious black smoke billowing from the hold."

"And your instincts and training kicked in."

"I guess. But the fire was all contained. A fifty-five-gallon drum of who knew what set to produce as much smoke as possible. Definitely not amateurs.

They robbed us blind. And they took Patrick as insurance. He was cutting up, laughing. Telling us he'd be okay. We were supposed to wait twenty-four hours. Then we could follow. And pick him up at a designated location. But when we got there…''

"He wasn't there," Sydney finished for him.

Three years, and the pain still ripped him apart. He swallowed thickly. "I don't know why I thought he would be. We could all ID the bastards. Patrick especially. They would never have been as successful as they obviously were if their MO had included releasing their hostages."

Ray was silent for several long, lonely heartbeats. He drew a shuddering breath. "I'm guessing they shot him and threw him to the sharks. That makes the most sense, considering in three years we haven't turned up so much as a shoelace.

"Goddamn. He was only twenty-two years old." Ray sat forward and dragged both hands down his face. "He was having the time of his life and then it was over. Just like that. I only hope it was fast. And that he didn't suffer."

"Oh, honey, don't do this to yourself." Sydney moved closer and eased down to sit in his lap, pressing both palms to his chest, as if she could absorb his hurt. "If I'd known the Caribbean reminded you so much of bad times, I could've had the crew take us anywhere."

"Yeah? And where would we have ended up?" Ray asked with a short laugh. "Floating twelve miles out to sea? Besides, I love the Caribbean. And being here actually helps me work through a lot of the bad stuff.'' A statement he hadn't realized was true until he put it into words.

Or maybe it was the feel of a soft woman in his lap that soothed his memories. He would drown in those compassionate blue eyes if he didn't lighten the mood. He tilted his head. ''Besides, I had to be sure wherever we went I'd get to see you in a bikini.''

''What?'' she asked in mock insult. ''You don't like me in a one-piece?''

''I like you any way I can get you. And right now I'm liking you a whole lot right where you are.''

''Unless I'm reading you wrong, Ray Coffey, that sounds like you're hitting on me.''

He didn't know how she could be reading him any way but right, because his lap was beginning to stir and harden. ''I don't make it a habit of hitting on defenseless women. And that's all I have to say about *that*.''

''Good,'' she said, and wrapped her arms around his neck. ''I'm glad we got that cleared up.''

He wasn't sure what exactly she now saw with more clarity, but he hoped she was telling him she wasn't the least bit defenseless. He draped one arm across her legs and moved his other hand into her hair. Not kissing her didn't even cross his mind.

Her lips pressed to his in tentative exploration. They weren't the lips he'd imagined. They were soft and slow-moving, testing their way, reliving, remembering, realizing that nothing was the same.

Her taste was richer, her scent a headier mix of perfume and arousal. And her subtle movements raised the stakes, an underlying question asking him if he wanted her. Even had she been blind, she wouldn't have needed braille. Not if her sense of touch had risen anywhere close to his heightened level.

The hand she had splayed over his chest she now moved up to hold his jaw still. As if he was going anywhere. But he let her keep him right where she wanted him, anyway. He liked that she wasn't defenseless. He also liked that she was bold, that she had no trouble feeling her way toward what she wanted.

She nipped lightly at his lower lip to let him know she wanted him to open up. He smiled and he opened, because he'd been waiting for this too long not to let her have things her way, any way. Whatever she wanted, he was patient.

The slats of the cedar chair creaked. A gentle breeze lifted strands of Sydney's hair, blowing it to tickle Ray's face. He caught a whiff of coconut, of wild grass, of air that blew in from the sea. The sky above was spotted with balls of cotton clouds and a moon that seemed to take up half of the tropical night.

Ray closed his eyes and went to heaven, sitting back and sitting still while Sydney used her tongue to feel her way through his mouth. The surface of his teeth, his lips, his palette, his cheeks. His texture and his taste and his own tongue, which she finally engaged.

She kissed as if it was an art, as if the more time she spent in methodical, paint-by-numbers practice the more pleasurable the sensory result. Ray wasn't sure his senses could take much more of the way she'd decided to ease her way into an embrace.

How was a man supposed to rein in a desire that

burned from the inside out, that made a joke out of the control he maintained over his emotions, that reminded him how human he was when he worked his ass off to be above and beyond? Ray was in trouble, big trouble, deep-down-to-the-bone trouble, and he wouldn't have it any other way.

Sydney's fingers on his face were cool, her lips on his warm. But her tongue mating with his was fire-hot and liquid in the way it flowed over and under, caressing and stroking and rubbing along his. He held her head fast and increased the pressure and intensity of the kiss, taking the embrace to another level when he moved his hand up her thigh to her belly before covering her breast.

The sound she made wasn't the least bit soft or sweet, but rather brutally hungry, and Ray couldn't help but lift his hips and grind against her. What he wanted was to grind against her while buried deep in her honeyed warmth, to have her grind back, finding the pressure, the angle, the rhythm of the stroke she needed to get off.

Her mouth was taking him to the edge, and she wasn't doing anything more than kissing his. Ray wasn't sure he'd ever known a kiss so incredibly, so amazingly arousing. And when Sydney moved her hand from his face to press against his where it covered her breast, he thought he was going to come right then and there.

"Sydney." He half muttered, half whispered her name into her mouth. She moved a breath away and he said, "This isn't working."

"Everything feels in working order to me." She wiggled her seat in his lap.

"That's what I'm talking about." He pressed his lips to hers firmly, kissed her with a hard and solidly aimed intent. He might be breaking off this contact, but the separation was to be only temporary.

He wondered if they could make it to his bedroom unseen. "I need to get out of this chair and stretch my, uh, legs."

She was slow to move, but she was gentle, which he greatly appreciated. Once she was back on her feet, he pushed up to his. He shook off what he could of his binding discomfort and then backed Sydney into the corner of the deck. She retreated until she ran into the railing. Then, bracing herself against it with her hands, she invitingly lifted her chin.

"About that time you're supposed to be finding us to spend together..." Ray let the thought trail as he moved in closer. He covered both of her hands with his—hers, so delicate and feminine, yet strong—and lowered his head. Time to take up where they'd left off.

"Sydney, Ray? You two up there?"

At Jess's shouted question, Sydney chuckled, then ducked out from under one of Ray's arms. He hung his head, staring at the deck between his feet and the empty space she'd left behind. He wasn't sure his luck could get any worse. But then he felt Sydney's hand in the center of his back.

"Up here, Jess," she called before she leaned in close to Ray and whispered, "Good things come to those who wait?"

"Are you asking me or telling me?" he growled back as Sydney headed for the staircase.

"Neither one," she said, waiting for Jess to finish

climbing up so she could climb down. She patted his shoulder as he walked past, then called back to Ray, "I'm making you a promise."

Ray watched her bobbing blond ponytail disappear, then he sank back into the cedar deck chair and, loud enough for an obviously curious Jess to hear, grumbled, "Women."

5

"So, Sydney. What else is there to do around here?"

Standing at the kitchen counter and sipping her first cup of coffee, Sydney glanced over at Doug who was shoveling the last of Auralie's cheese-and-bean omelette into his mouth. "Are you saying you're bored already?"

"Hell, no. But I'm still waterlogged from yesterday. I was thinking of doing some sightseeing. Something that's dry. At least until my ears finish draining." He wiggled the finger he'd stuck in his ear.

"Just like a kid." Sitting at Doug's side, Kinsey shook her head, her feet on her chair and her knees drawn to her chest, while she cradled and sipped from her own stoneware mug. Dozens of tiny blond braids hung down her back, the result of Poe's handiwork from the evening before. "You think you're going to miss out and you ended up overdoing."

"I *am* a kid. Or at least I'm a kid when I'm on vacation." Pushing away from his plate, Doug sat back and stretched.

"You're a kid all the time. Just ask any of our contractors." Anton came into the room in time to catch Doug's declaration. "Why do you think the firm is called Neville & Storey, rather than Storey & Neville?''

Arms high overhead, Doug glanced behind him at his partner's approach. ''I thought we decided to put the brains second, so the brawn would get some of the glory, too.''

''Yeah, that's it,'' Anton said, reaching out and jerking back Doug's chair, nearly sending him tumbling to the floor.

Doug caught his balance in the nick of time...and with a little help from Kinsey, who flew forward and grabbed him by one wrist just as he reached out flailing wildly. He gave Anton a one-eyed glare, then leaned forward and kissed Kinsey full on the mouth.

Pulling away and leaving her momentarily stunned, Doug smacked his lips and headed for the kitchen. ''Mmm. Coffee. I think I'll have a cup.''

''Coffee?'' Kinsey fairly screeched, looking from her cup to Doug's departure as if weighing her need for caffeine against the pleasure of seeing the liquid splattered across his back. ''I've been trying to get you to kiss me for months and, when you finally do, all you can say is 'Coffee'?''

Doug had been halfway to the kitchen and now Sydney watched as he jolted to a stop. The choice between coffee and Kinsey wasn't one that took him more than half a shake. He quickly put himself in reverse and returned to the table, grabbing Kinsey's coffee mug in one hand—prying it free from her death grip—and taking hold of her upper arm in his other.

Then he propelled her from her chair and toward the villa's front door, disappearing while Sydney looked on with a sigh and remembered last night's kiss she'd shared with Ray. A kiss that had been a long time in coming and had been cut too short too soon. She'd barely had time to savor his texture or rediscover his taste; she'd been too busy offering him what he seemed to need, what had been her pleasure to give.

Now, of course, here she was again surrounded by friends whom she wryly wished would find an island of their own. She couldn't even find private time to *think* about Ray, much less time to spend with him alone. Her plans to work him out of her system didn't stand a chance of coming to pass if she never found time to spend with him alone.

And if she didn't accomplish her goal while on their shared vacation, she wasn't sure when she'd have another opportunity.

Work was going to be a bear when she got back to the States. Soon it would be holiday season, and the gIRL-gEAR partners had to prepare for yet another restructuring and the launch of Chloe's mentoring program. Business had to be Sydney's number-one priority at all times, well above her personal life.

The success of gIRL-gEAR meant more to her than her partners would ever know. More than was probably smart for her to let it mean. The company offered her the acceptance she'd never found as the Ice Queen, the respect she'd never earned from her free-spirited mother Vegas Ford—a mother who'd called her only daughter a gloomy Eeyore.

But most of all, gIRL-gEAR was Sydney's baby. A baby that fed off the creative types with which she'd surrounded herself, but a baby nurtured from day one by her business acumen. The success of the company rested solely on her shoulders. And had nothing to do with her world-famous artist mother or her venture-capitalist father.

Sydney shook off the thoughts as Anton, having poured himself a cup of coffee, took up his place beside her and stared after the exiting duo of Kinsey and Doug. Giving Anton a small shrug, Sydney lifted her mug. Interesting, finding out that Doug and Kinsey hadn't yet kissed.

That left only Jess and Poe as the possible first-floor veranda culprits from the other night.

Unless it had been Doug and Poe.

Or Kinsey and Jess.

Damn. Sydney was no closer to solving the mystery than she'd been yesterday. She slid a glance toward Anton. "Where's Lauren?"

Blowing across the surface of the steaming brew, Anton shrugged. "Still sleeping, I guess. I'm bunking with Doug, remember? You should've asked Kinsey before she went chasing after him."

"Chasing after Doug? If you think Kinsey was the one doing the chasing, no wonder you and Lauren can't get it together," Sydney said, treading where she had no business treading but doing so, anyway, wanting to see how Anton would react, wanting to see if he shared any of Lauren's confusion or if he had his mind made up.

"What're you talking about?" He frowned down into his coffee mug, then down at Sydney. "Doug might've been the one on his feet, but that doesn't mean he wasn't the one being pursued. You heard what Kinsey said. About wanting him to kiss her. That's chasing in my book.''

No wonder relationships were in so much trouble, Sydney mused, what with the way men and women saw things through such hormonally tinted lenses. She sipped at her coffee, swallowed, then opened her mouth to answer.

Anton cut her off. ''Besides, I'd like to think that whatever is going on between me and Lauren is between me and Lauren. Though I have to admit I wasn't sure at first how it was going to work out having both her and Poe on this trip.'' Anton hesitated. ''They seem to be getting along.''

Sydney nodded. Men were so cute when they were dealing with women. ''I think they are. I know they've talked.''

''About me?''

She glanced up and over and smiled. Anton's expression was the epitome of a nervous little boy waiting to find out if he'd been picked for the team. She couldn't help feel a touch of pity, though her first loyalties had to lie with Lauren.

''You probably need to take that up with Lauren. Or with Poe.''

''Take what up with Poe?'' Poe asked, walking into the room, scrunching her head of black hair with her fingers as if she'd abandoned conventional grooming while on vacation.

The swimsuit she wore was one Sydney recognized from Kinsey's gO gIRL sportswear collection, a two-piece set of low-cut shorts and a matching halter top. The color was a rich jade-green, a perfect complement to Poe's complexion.

"Wow." Eyes wide, Sydney shook her head. "Has Kinsey seen you in that suit?"

"What suit? Where? Oh, Poe! You look fantastic," Kinsey said, returning through the same door from which she'd exited earlier. Doug followed, looking glassy-eyed and more than a little bit frustrated.

Poe turned to model the suit, stopping and raising both brows as she caught sight of the duo. Her hands went to her hips. "Okay. What have you two been up to? What am I missing? And why do I feel so left out?"

"I seem to recall you getting yours a couple of nights ago," Jess said from where he stood in the door to the hallway. He crossed the main room and slapped Poe on the butt as he walked by. She yelped and rubbed her fanny, then frowned at Jess as he leaned across the kitchen's wide counter.

Grabbing the coffeepot and two mugs, he slid both back with him, pouring first for Poe and then for himself. He grinned shamelessly, and Poe, taking her cup, first rolled her eyes, then glared. "Thanks, Jess. The way you put that…now everyone's going to think more went on between us than that truth-or-dare kiss."

"And here I had my hopes up," Sydney said, halfway teasing and halfway disappointed. For a minute there she'd been so sure she'd finally fingered the mystery lovers.

One eye narrowed beneath one raised brow, Jess added cream and sugar to his mug and asked, "You're not playing matchmaker, are you, Sydney?"

She looked from Jess to Poe to Doug to Kinsey and finally up to Anton. Keeping a grin from her face was next to impossible, so she didn't even try. "Why would I need to play matchmaker when all of you are doing fine on your own?"

"Very funny," Kinsey said to Sydney while patting Doug on the head and tucking him back into his chair at the table. "You sit right here and recover, honey. I'll get you that coffee you needed."

Doug opened his mouth, but nothing came out, so he shut it again. Anton and Jess looked on with a combination of envy and offense taken on behalf of all mankind. Sydney looked at Poe, shrugged and decided then and there that the entire world was ruled by sex.

Not such a bad thing really. Except in this case where it seemed she was the only one who wasn't finding the opportunities everyone else seemed to be finding. Or at least the opportunity *one* couple had found, making her admittedly as envious as she was curious. And where was Ray, anyway?

"Kinsey, is Lauren still sleeping?"

"Yeah. She's being a lazybones this morning." Kinsey filled the mug she'd found and carried it back to Doug. "But then, I didn't finish the movie last night, so I was out like a light when she finally came to bed."

Sydney herself hadn't stayed up long at all after leaving Jess and Ray on the deck. She thought she remembered hearing Poe come to bed and had tried to wake up, wanting to talk to the other woman. After all, getting to know her had been the reason she'd invited Poe along in the first place.

If it wasn't one plan going awry, it was another. She turned her attention to Jess. "What about Ray?"

"What about Ray?" Jess echoed, his elbow propped on Poe's convenient shoulder. "You taking morning roll call or something?"

"No, but Doug was interested in land-based activities, and I thought I'd fill everyone in at the same time." Sydney moved to the sink and ran enough water to wash what breakfast dishes remained, since Auralie had moved to cleaning bathrooms and linens.

Jess shook his head. "Ray's been gone awhile. But I doubt he's gone far because, hey, there's not too far anyone can go here."

Sydney waited until he'd drained his cup, then grabbed it and dunked it in the sink of soapy water. "Are you complaining?"

"Hell, no. I like working within prescribed limits." He stretched, then lowered both arms, draping one casually across Poe's back and tucking his fingers into her ribs. "Takes off the pressure of seeing what I can get away with."

Poe slipped out from beneath, twisting around and pulling Jess's arm up into the center of his back until he grimaced and cried uncle. "Gives a new meaning to pressure, eh, big boy?"

Sydney was vacationing in a zoo, that was all there was to it. "If any of you are interested, I am heading down to the south beach, where there's a lagoon. Menga has already set up the umbrellas and there are floats stored in the cabana. I'm taking a book and a beach blanket.

"If that's still too much water, Doug," Sydney added, taking in Doug's waterlogged expression, "the trail to the pelican nesting ground runs right past the beach and it's only a ten-minute walk."

Doug nodded. "Birds I can probably handle."

"Actually you can't handle them at all. It's against the rules."

"Ha, ha, ha," Doug said just as a sleepy-eyed Lauren made her way into the room.

"What's against the rules?" she asked, accepting the coffee Anton poured for her and rising on her toes to share a quick kiss. "Mmm. Sweet."

It was definitely time to get out of the kitchen, Sydney grumped to herself, finishing up the last mug and drying her hands. All this touchy-feely business going on and Ray nowhere to be found. Her plans for a hedonistic vacation fling seemed to have been flung far and wide.

"Cavorting with the wildlife," Jess replied to Lauren, then pushed off the counter and headed for the stairs to the second-floor bedroom suites. "I'm going for shoes. It's time to work off this vacation."

STRANGELY ENOUGH, when Sydney got to the south beach, she finally found Ray. He'd managed to discover the lagoon and the cove all on his own. He'd obviously discovered the cabana, as well, because he was making full use of one of the stored floats.

Poe, who'd decided to forgo the pelicans and settle for the book-and-umbrella routine, had accompanied Sydney to the beach. Both women spread their blankets over the clean, white sand.

Sydney couldn't even dredge up the energy to be annoyed at sharing the secluded beach with Poe, instead of being alone with Ray. Yes, she intended to seduce her prey. But she also had gIRL-gEAR business to take care of with Poe.

Once settled on the blankets, totes with sunscreen and bottled water and paperback bestsellers nearby, neither woman did anything but sit and relax. Poe leaned back on her elbows. Sydney leaned back on her palms. The water in the small lagoon was still and clear.

Ray floated on his back in a circular tube, his arms stretched overhead, his legs dangling in the water, his sculpted belly flat and the material of his swim trunks bulging below. Dark sunglasses were wrapped around his head, hiding his eyes and his expression. He hadn't waved; she wondered if he'd seen them arrive, and so she lifted a hand.

He raised his in return, answering that one question, leaving unanswered myriad others. Was he watching her now? Was he remembering the kiss they'd shared last night? What was he thinking? Did he have any idea how finding him here, seeing him relaxed and rested and touched by the light of the sun, sent her pulse skittering?

Sydney wondered if Poe was as caught up by the visual as she was. Because, of all the men sharing their island vacation, there was just something about Ray Coffey that set him apart from the others. At least to Sydney's way of thinking. She cast what she hoped was a surreptitious glance at Poe, only to find her with her head back and her raised face seeking the warmth of the sun.

"Don't worry. I know he's off-limits."

Poe's cryptic comment caused Sydney to raise a brow. "Are you talking about Ray?"

"Isn't that who you're sitting there fantasizing about? Not that I blame you," Poe added, tilting her head in Sydney's direction, but still not making eye contact, which would've been difficult, anyway, with the two of them wearing their sleek Oakleys.

Sydney pressed her lips together. Were her thoughts really that obvious? Or was Poe only hazarding a heat-seeking guess? Well, two could play *that* game, Sydney mused with a private smirk. "I'm surprised you've had time to take notice of Ray, what with Jess monopolizing so much of your time."

"He is a doll, isn't he?" Poe's grin spoke volumes about the road her own thoughts had taken. "Trust me. After that truth-or-dare kiss? I did a quick evaluation of his fling potential."

"And?"

Poe gave a small, noncommittal shrug. "And I'm still evaluating. Vacation flings are so much easier and definitely less messy when both parties go their own way at the end of the trip. I loathe complications."

Sydney hadn't thought about that, about the tricky situation she'd find herself in seeing Ray on any kind of regular basis once they were back in the States.

Since his return to Houston last year, their occasional interaction had only served to heighten the tension between them. She'd continued to wonder, to fantasize, to evoke the tiniest details of that night they'd spent together. Details like his texture and his taste.

She'd had no idea, at eighteen, that a man's bare skin could be so soft, his body hair so baby fine, his scent so intoxicating, his taste equally so. There in that cheap hotel bed, she'd buried her nose against him, breathed fully and breathed deep. And she'd remembered. That night on the veranda, she'd remembered.

She'd never stopped to realize what it would mean to replace those memories with others. Adult memories. Recent memories. Memories that she wouldn't revisit with a virgin's naiveté but with a woman's understanding and appreciation of what she could share with a man.

So what exactly did she want to share with this man? Was it really the simple fling she'd been working for weeks to convince herself she wanted? Or now, after feeling his hands on her body that night on the veranda, after experiencing his kiss last night on the deck, was she thinking of wanting more than their time on this island allowed?

One touch, one kiss. A slow crescendo building toward the fulfillment of her fantasy. She was growing anxious, that was all. Once they made love, once she proved to herself that he was only a man and no different from any other, her mind would be clear of Ray Coffey, and life would get back to normal, back to business.

So why was she thinking about more? How could she possibly be wondering if she'd ever get enough?

"Besides," Poe went on, waving one hand in a welcome interruption to Sydney's musings. "As hot as Jess is, he's still so…young."

Funny, but Poe's remarks tied into what Lauren had said only yesterday about Poe's being the type of woman Sydney's father needed in his life. Sydney couldn't necessarily argue about the type; she just wasn't sure Poe was the one.

"Jess is what? Four years younger than you?" As opposed to Nolan, who was a decade older than Poe.

"Something like that, I imagine. But it's not so much the actual years as it is the attitude. I'm almost thirty-two. I don't look at the world now the same way I did at, say, twenty-eight."

"You make it sound like the two of you are worlds apart." Sydney paused to let that sink in before adding, "Jess is probably not quite the boy toy you seem to think."

"Hmm," was all Poe gave in response before pushing up off her elbows and digging in her tote for her bottle of water. After taking a drink, she cast a glance at Sydney. "I thought Jess had a thing going on with Melanie, anyway."

"I know they've dated, but I think they're just good friends," Sydney replied, glad to see that Poe had taken Mel's feelings into consideration. The gIRL-gEAR partners shared an unparalleled closeness, and making Poe a part of that team would be a much easier transition for all involved if they knew she saw things with the same eyes.

"Hmm," Poe hummed again. "I suppose all I can do is see what happens, then, right? Though I still think it would be easier to find myself a nice buff local lad to play with."

Chuckling, Sydney shook her head. "You are so bad."

Poe heaved a theatrical sigh. "I do try. It makes life so much more exciting. However—" she held up one finger "—I am fully aware that being good has its perks, as well. Catching flies with honey and all that."

"You know," Sydney said, "Chloe insists you are not the bitch you pretend to be."

"Well, damn. And here I was working so hard at my image."

"Why would you want us to think you're something that you're not?"

"Why does anyone lie?" Poe shrugged. "To hide the ugly truth, right?"

Sydney should have been used to Poe's dramatic nature by now, but she still caught herself doing a mental double take. "It might be. If one had an ugly truth to hide. Which I don't believe you do."

"Everyone has a secret, Sydney Ford." Poe slipped her sunglasses down her nose and met Sydney's gaze head on. "Yours just happens to be a lot hunkier than any I might have."

All Sydney could do was blink. Here she'd been prepared to discuss Poe's impending promotion within gIRL-gEAR, and the woman had to blow a cover Sydney thought was so convincing. Not to mention remind her of a more immediate concern.

So immediate, in fact, that when she turned from Poe to glance out toward Ray, where he floated on the quiet surface of the water, Sydney's breath caught hard and fast. He wasn't floating any longer. He was, in fact, walking up the beach toward her, dripping wet, water glistening in diamond drops all over his incredible body.

He was tall and he was broad, and he filled her vision as he moved lithely over the sand. He stopped when he was but two feet away. For a minute he did nothing but look down. His eyes were hidden behind sunshades, so Sydney couldn't see the sparkle in his eyes. But she knew it was there. The teasing quirk at the corner of his solemn mouth gave him away.

"Ladies," he said, and held out a hand to Sydney. She accepted and got to her feet, dusting sand from the seat of her yellow bikini.

"Hello, Ray." Poe returned to reclining on her elbows. "It's nice to see you."

Sydney wanted to roll her eyes. But then Ray said, "It's nice to be seen," and tugged his glasses down enough to give Poe a wink. Sydney managed to resist smacking him on the shoulder. And then all she could do was let out a loud, "Whoop!" as Ray hoisted her into his arms and headed back for the lagoon to the tune of Poe's call of, "You two have fun!"

Ray glanced down at Sydney and raised a brow above the rims of his shades. "Your suit is waterproof, right?"

"It's a swimsuit, Ray. It's made to get wet." Oh, but he felt good. One arm around her back, the other beneath her legs, his chest warm and hard and solid at her shoulder. She laced her hands behind his neck and held on tightly, refusing to be alarmed by his grin, which was borderline dastardly.

The grin widened. "Just making sure it's not one of those fancy look-but-don't-touch numbers."

Please touch, she wanted to say, but instead, she waited for the dunking she was sure he'd give her. Surprisingly enough, he didn't. But what he did certainly grabbed her attention in ways a dunking would've failed to do.

He settled his body back into the center of the circular float and settled her body on top. The float was sturdy and easily held them both. Ray had once again draped his arms overhead, giving Sydney the broad expanse of his chest to lie back on.

She kept one hand on her stomach. The other she trailed over the side, dangling her fingers in the water. Her legs tangled in and out of Ray's, but it was her backside in the dip of his lap causing her the most grief. She wanted to wiggle. She wanted to be still. She wasn't sure which want she wanted the most.

"I've been thinking, Sydney."

Ray's voice rumbled through her rib cage. She waited for the shudders to fade, savoring the deep echo before she replied, "That can be dangerous, you know."

"Watch it, woman. I can still change my mind about sharing this float."

"I don't remember asking to share your float."

They drifted silently for another moment or two, until Sydney started to wonder if she could maneuver with enough dexterity to dunk Ray while staying high and marginally dry. But she was enjoying his lap way too much to act on the renegade thought.

"Ray?"

"Hmm?"

"You've been thinking?"

"I've been thinking that you've been making promises you can't keep."

"Is that so?"

"Yep. It's so."

"I suppose you're talking about finding time for us to spend together?"

"That would be the one."

"Well, we're together now."

"We're together with Poe."

"Hmm," Sydney mumbled, pulling her hand through the water enough to turn the float beachward. "Poe's gone."

"Yeah. Some friend you are, abandoning her like that."

"I got...an offer I couldn't refuse." She'd started to say, "a better offer," but had stopped the words before they'd rushed out. She wasn't sure why.

"Damn straight. And a better offer, at that."

"Oh, yeah? Says who?" She kicked her feet, splashing water over their legs.

"Says the man who wants to get you naked in the worst possible way."

"Oh. That man," Sydney said, barely able to get the words past the rush of desire working to close off her throat. Especially when she felt Ray begin to stir and harden further. Neither one of their suits was made of anything but the thinnest fabric, and he had to know she could feel him.

She wasn't sure what move to make next. And was glad when he let her off the hook. "We're three days into this trip, Sydney."

She sighed. "I know."

"And I'm usually a very patient man. But not this time. I've been waiting for you for eight years." He lowered one arm and splayed his hand flat across her belly. "Eight years is a helluva long time."

And didn't she know it. Waiting to touch him, to learn him, to know him. Waiting to have his hands on her body the way she had them now. "You're right. It has been. And you'd better be worth all this waiting."

Ray stilled beneath her. His second hand joined the

first, both measuring the span of her stomach. And then he chuckled, and Sydney felt the tickle scuttle the length of her back.

"I could say the same thing to you."

"You could." She smiled to herself. "But you won't."

This time he laughed and the sound rolled up from deep in his belly. His hands squeezed her waist. "You know, Sydney Ford, there's one other thing I want to do in the worst possible way."

"You wouldn't dare," she said sensing that the time for that dunking had arrived.

"Oh, yeah?" he answered, and hoisted her, squealing, into the lagoon.

6

THE NEXT MORNING found Sydney in high spirits. Between their impromptu water fights, she and Ray had floated away most of the previous afternoon at the south beach lagoon—at least until others had discovered their paradise and crashed their private party. Today she'd made an early escape, needing a breather from the constant company, time with her own thoughts, and hopefully time alone with Ray.

Listening to the summer thunderstorm rolling in from offshore, Sydney slowed her steps, enjoying the feel of the loose sand shifting beneath her feet and the sharp metallic bite to the air. Low-hanging clouds, bellies pregnant with rain, scudded in to obliterate the afternoon sun. But the breeze was still warm and soothing, and Sydney knew when the rain washed over the island, it would be warm, as well.

She so loved the heightened sense of calm before the storm. She rubbed her hands up and down her bare arms...not for warmth but because the electrical charge in the air tickled her skin. She wasn't sure she'd make it back to the villa before the storm broke, but halfway between here and there, on one of the island's two landscaped beaches, was an open-air pagoda sitting in a cluster of coconut palms.

She wasn't sure where the rest of the group would

find shelter from the approaching midday cloudburst. Lauren and Anton had gone to the mainland with Menga Duarte this morning on the caretaker's trip for additional supplies. The couple had plans to tour several Mayan ruins and wouldn't have any trouble finding cover from the rain.

Sydney wasn't sure if they were working to reconcile or if they'd only called a temporary truce. She supposed the reason for their togetherness wasn't half as important as the fact that they were together and, at least on some level, facing rather than avoiding the conflict keeping them apart. More than any couple she knew, those two belonged together, and she had her fingers crossed that her ''butting in'' would not go awry.

Doug, Jess, Kinsey and Poe had all gone snorkeling at the north end of the island. Apparently Doug was no longer waterlogged, because he couldn't wait to get wet. And scorched. He was definitely working on a major tan and the deep bronze of his skin was doing a fine job setting off the sheen of his sun-bleached hair. He wore the surfer look well. And Kinsey had not failed to take notice.

Jess and Poe were noticing each other, too. But after talking with Poe yesterday, Sydney wasn't sure all the noticing in the world would get either of them anywhere. Poe had seemed to quietly retreat, leaving Jess hanging in his own confusion with not much to say. What he did say was that he was having the time of his life, a time made even better without the added complication of having a woman along. Sydney doubted anyone believed him.

Sydney didn't think Ray had accompanied the fun-loving group, though he had left the villa this morning around the same time. He hadn't had much of anything to say over breakfast. He hadn't really stayed for breakfast, as a matter of fact. For some reason yesterday's playful romp in the lagoon seemed to have changed things between them. But she couldn't put a finger on what. Or why.

He'd poured himself a cup of Auralie's coffee, grabbed a banana from the fruit bowl and then he'd walked down the length of the private pier, wearing a pair of bright orange board shorts and a sleeveless black T-shirt. Sydney had stood in the villa's front doorway and sipped her own coffee, wondering what he had on his mind.

She hadn't been able to gauge his mood, and that bothered her, distracted her, reminded her again how important it was that she keep their relationship confined to this island and, quite frankly, to sex. Nolan had taught her to put business before anything, if she expected to succeed, and never to make choices based on her heart, instead of her head.

She'd spent her life following her father's advice. Or at least she'd tried. For the most part, she'd succeeded. gIRL-gEAR spoke to her dedication and commitment and sound business plan. It was only last year that she'd stepped foot outside of her strictly drawn boundaries and gone to Nolan for personal reasons, emotional reasons. A mistake she should've known better than to make. One that had left her reeling, left her raw at his betrayal, left her sick at having let down a friend.

A fat drop of rain fell with a splat on her bare shoulder. A second followed, then a third, and the pagoda was still a hundred yards away. She wouldn't mind a thorough soaking, but she broke into a run, anyway, because running for shelter from the island's summer storms had always been a game she and her mother had played.

She hadn't thought of those happier times in far too long and was laughing when she reached the covered shelter and set about lowering the protective screens. She was on the back side of the three-walled enclosure when her laughter stilled, when her memories moved several years forward, when the rain and the isolation took on an ambiance of intimacy. Because jogging toward the pagoda from the other direction was Ray.

He ducked inside just as she let go of the last cord and the third screen rolled to the ground. They were both dripping wet and slightly out of breath. Sydney wasn't going to question serendipity. She was too glad to see him to analyze the way the Fates had come together. And she sure wasn't going to analyze why she was so glad.

"Hi," she said, shaking the water from her bare arms, wishing for a towel or even the dry hem of a shirt. But neither her bright yellow bikini top or her green-and-yellow drawstring shorts offered a solution. She settled for wiping the water away with her palms. "I thought maybe you'd ended up going snorkeling with the others."

Ray shook his head, then shook it again and sent water droplets flying. He scrubbed his hands back over his head. "I walked back to the pelican nesting area and ended up circling most of the island. This is some place Nolan's got here. His own wildlife refuge and everything.''

''I don't think anything has ever made me realize how lucky I was growing up as this island has.'' Sydney drew in a deep breath and faced the open side of the pagoda, the side facing the sea. ''Did you know I actually had my sixteenth birthday party here?''

''I heard the rumors. Heard that that party caused you more than a little grief that year.''

Funny, but she'd actually forgotten about the stir caused by the flack the six girls had received for the unexcused absence. An absence due to mechanical problems forcing the cancellation of their return flight to Houston.

Sydney had sat through more than one lecture about district policies applying to all students, no matter their economic advantage—or their family's endowment to the school. But it was Izzy Leighton who'd suffered the most.

The missed day disqualified her from an interscholastic competition she'd been almost guaranteed to win. A competition with a scholarship she'd been counting on to cover the bulk of her tuition to Rice University. None of Nolan's appeals or those of Izzy's parents had changed the school board's mind.

Sydney had sworn for years she'd make it up to her friend. And last year she'd tried, ending up with nothing for her efforts but an estrangement from the father who'd sworn he'd never let her down. Eyes closed, Sydney took a deep breath. Then she forced a smile and turned back to Ray.

''You know what? I don't want to talk about the past. I want to talk about now. I want to enjoy this vacation and have fun and forget about work and about all the problems I'll have to deal with once we get home.''

''Including the problems with your father?'' he asked, his hands at his hips, both brows arched.

He said it as though it was his business to know, to find out what had gone on to cause the rift. But she couldn't give him the details, because he wouldn't understand. No one who hadn't lived in her shoes would ever understand. The explanation was tied up with the fact that she was the daughter of multimillionaires Nolan and Vegas Ford.

She gave a small sad shake of her head, blew out a short snort of breath. And then walked several steps away.

''You're shutting me out, Sydney. Don't shut me out.'' Ray walked up close behind her. ''Anyone who has been around you this last year knows you barely speak to Nolan. But no one can figure out why. And, yeah. Everyone is curious. Because whatever is going on is obviously one-sided.''

''Yes, it's one-sided,'' Sydney said, grinding her teeth and feeling the first stirrings of the stress headache she was learning to live with. ''I feel Nolan betrayed me. He disagrees. And I'd like to leave it at that, if you don't mind.''

And quite frankly, she didn't care if he did mind. She moved farther away from Ray, staring out into the rain and watching the drops hammer the sand. This wasn't his business. This was between her and her father. And, unfortunately, her mother.

And just when Sydney's life had finally hit an incredibly satisfying and successful stride, too. gIRL-gEAR was experiencing amazing success, growing and expanding beyond anything she or her partners had ever imagined. Her personal life was on hold, which was fine and all part of her grand master plan.

So why did things with her father have to go south the way they had? Nolan had always been her rock—

"Hey." Ray settled his hands on her shoulders. "Sydney, honey, listen to me. Whatever you have going on with Nolan is your business. You're right. But I've gotten to know your father recently. He made a huge donation to one of the firefighter funds after the attacks last year, and we've talked a lot. About the things I've seen. And about Patrick.

"We've become close, and I care about him as a friend. He hates this estrangement. He says he understands how you feel. And, no," Ray said, cutting off her objection, "he hasn't divulged any details. He respects your privacy and your feelings. But he's not a happy man right now."

"Well, I'm not exactly a happy woman. What Nolan did can't be undone. It's something I'm going to have to live with." And no one had any idea how much she hurt.

She'd always been able to turn to her father for anything. Anything. And losing that touchstone, that bedrock defining who she was and where she came from... Sydney shivered. For the first time in her entire life she was free-falling. No parachute. No safety net. Only the life lessons she'd learned at her father's feet. And she didn't know if she'd learned enough to make it on her own.

Ray began to massage her shoulders, kneading muscles and tendons that were often tight with everyday stress. Not so today. Today relaxation came easily, once she ground her train of thought to a halt and turned her focus outward, to the here and the now. Then there was only Ray's skin on her skin, his strong hands testing and measuring her flesh and her response until her stress became something only Ray could take away.

Rain pelted the pagoda, drumming overhead in a primal rhythm, slapping against the sand and farther out onto a Caribbean whipped into frothy waves by the winds. Sydney wanted to be angry at Ray for dredging up her problems with her father. But she couldn't find even a hint of anger to draw on. Not because doing so would interfere with her plans, but because what she felt standing there beneath Ray's hands left her speechless and unable to feel anything beyond the physical bliss of his touch.

He moved closer, bringing his body a hairbreadth from pressing solidly to hers. She could feel the heat from his thighs warm her skin through the thin cotton of her shorts. Her back, bare but for the narrow tie of her bikini top, leeched the heat from his torso.

His hands continued to rub, to stroke, to raise the temperature of her skin and blood. The way he so easily aroused her was part of the reason he kept her unnerved. And the whole of the reason she was here.

Yet when faced with the full effect Ray had on her body, Sydney could only close her eyes. She was unable to resist. Or to think. How could she get him out of her system when she couldn't form a coherent thought the minute he had her in his hands?

"I want to make you happy, Sydney." Ray's warm

breath brushed the skin at her nape. "Will you let me make you happy?"

Oh, God. How was she supposed to answer when she'd forgotten where she'd left her voice? Not to mention her wit, her common sense, her logic and rationale. All she knew was her desire. And so she closed her eyes and said, "Yes."

An aroused groan deep in Ray's throat vibrated through the palms of his hands as he skated them down Sydney's bare arms, slicking away the sheen of moisture still coating her skin. His touch warmed her, excited her, raised gooseflesh and the hairs on her nape. Her breasts tightened. Her nipples beaded into taut pebbles. Her sex grew swollen and aching and damp.

All of this, this response, so intensely real, so immediate and sweet…and he'd done nothing yet but caress her from shoulder to wrist, wrist to shoulder, his big hands cupping her limbs gently before meeting at the back of her neck. He pressed his thumbs there and let his fingers wrap around to tease the skin of her throat.

She lifted her chin, inviting further exploration, and he ran the backs of his fingers along her jaw, traced the shells of both ears, blowing softly at her hairline as he threaded his hands into her hair. He massaged her scalp, her temples, the base of her skull, and Sydney was certain her temperature was approaching the point where she would melt into the sand around his feet. Nothing had ever, ever felt this good.

She moaned her approval, her appreciation, and then Ray laid his forearm across her collarbone and pulled her back into his chest. His arm was a welcome pressure. The damp fabric of his shirt was cool at first contact until heated by the beat of his heart and the rush of blood beneath the surface of his skin.

Even his breath offered a sweep of warmth that heightened her sense of touch. She felt like a live wire, sizzling and sparking in the rain. Sand popped up like divots and the sea water rippled, circle upon circle spreading over the foaming waves.

The moment took eroticism to heights Sydney had never known. And then Ray moved his free hand, skimming his palm over one breast, then the other, touching nothing but the barest surface of the bright yellow suit covering her skin, nothing but the suit and the tips of both nipples, one, two, his palm circling until she wanted to reach back and untie the strings of her top and give him her bare skin.

Ray seemed to know what she wanted—and seemed determined to refuse her unspoken request. He kept his forearm in place, bracing and holding her still. His lips moved to her neck, to the skin beneath her ear where he nibbled and nipped, where he kissed, where he blew a stream of heat over skin dampened by his teasing tongue.

Oh, God. She was about to come unglued. Nerve endings hummed along the surface of her limbs and the bare skin of her belly and her back, still pressed to Ray's solid strength. The screens she'd lowered on three sides of the pagoda kept most of the rain at bay, but from the fourth side, the open side, the side she faced, mist blew in and settled on her skin, kissing her face, wetting the surface of her clothing while the steam Ray was raising on her body moistened the material from the inside out.

She shivered and his lips sucked lightly at her shoulder and his free hand, oh, his hand… His finger finally slipped beneath her suit, where he took a nipple between forefinger and thumb and rolled and pinched and tugged until Sydney dropped her head back onto his chest and moaned.

"Good?" he asked, his voice a husky, throaty sound.

"You have no idea." How could he? How could he know what he was doing to her?

"I have a pretty good one. We've done this before, remember?"

"You have a hell of a memory, Ray Coffey. I'm beginning to think you know more about me than I know about myself." She had no idea how he knew, but his knowledge was unquestionable, his instinct right on. Moisture seeped into the fabric of her shorts and she squirmed.

"I don't know half as much as I want to. Not yet." He continued to hold her close to his body. He continued to work his hand beneath the triangle of material covering her breast.

A shudder ran the length of her body. She dug her feet into the sand, lowered her hands to her sides and reached back, wrapping her fingers into the loose fabric of Ray's shorts. She knew he wasn't going anywhere, but still she held on.

She had to hold on, especially now, because he'd moved his hand lower, down her belly where he splayed his fingers, his hand so large he reached from one side of her waist to the other, as if measuring, testing the texture of her skin. She pulled in a sharp breath as his hand slid lower, his fingers loosening the drawstring and slipping beneath her shorts.

And he didn't stop there, but sent his exploring hand lower into her barely there panties, which were embarrassingly damp between her legs. She wanted him to know what he did to her, the extent to which he aroused her, but the physical evidence seemed too private to share.

Ray thought differently and said so. "Do you know I can smell you? I can smell the rain and the sea, but I can also smell how wet you are."

Sydney couldn't find her voice to reply. All she could do was stand still and spread her legs wide to accommodate Ray's hand. He was using two fingers, only two fingers, on either side of her clit, squeezing the hard knot of nerves from either side, stroking up and down, right there beneath the band of her panties and no deeper.

She wanted him as far between her legs as he could reach. But all he did was play in her closely trimmed patch of hair and over the plump lips of her sex. He never parted her folds, he never slipped a finger into the crevice. He only fingered her with the lightest of butterfly touches, pressing on either side of the swollen bud until Sydney thought she would die from needing release.

She swallowed hard and moaned, digging her fingers through the fabric of Ray's trunks and into his thighs. "What are you doing to me?"

"I hope I'm making you feel good. I hope I'm making you happy." He strung a trail of open-mouth kisses along her shoulder to her neck, the arm pressed across her collarbone drifting lower, coming to rest on her rib cage just beneath her breasts.

Sydney couldn't stand it any longer. She worked a hand between their bodies and pulled on the strings holding her top in place. The scraps of bright yellow fell free, exposing her to the mist of warm rain and the warm air and the heat from Ray's arm. She was on her way to heaven. Ray moaned, the rumble rolling through his chest and into Sydney's back. She felt his response to the tips of her toes.

"God, you're beautiful." He pulled his hand from her panties and cupped the full weight of both breasts, hugging her back and close to his body. "I don't know if I can get enough of you. I want to do so many things…"

He let the sentence trail. Sydney, aroused beyond belief, picked it up. "Tell me. Tell me what you want to do. I want to hear you say it."

The sound he made was half chuckle, half roar of pain. He released her breasts and wrapped both his arms around her middle. He hugged her close, his cheek to her cheek. "You like to hear a man talk dirty?"

She shook her head. "Not a man. You. I want to hear it from you."

"God, Sydney. Do you have any idea what you're doing to me?"

"Tell me," she whispered. "Show me."

He took one of her hands, guided their joined fingers between their bodies and closed her hold around his erection. "Feel that? That's what you do to me. No woman has ever made me ache like this. No woman has ever made me this hard."

Hard barely began to describe what Sydney held in her hand. He was hugely erect, turgid and swollen beyond belief. He was long and impressively thick. None of this was what she remembered.

She wanted him between her legs. But they were in an empty pagoda with a floor of sand, no walls, no furniture, nothing to use for support. And she certainly hadn't thought to bring a condom when she'd set out this morning.

But they were both in desperate need of relief and she was in no state of mind or body to be honorable or disciplined. She wanted to come. She wanted to make him come. And she was ready to act the part of the spoiled little rich girl if it meant she would get her way.

She started to turn in his arms, only to have Ray hold her in place. "Ray, please. Let's go back to the villa. To bed. I don't care about the rain. We can make love in the shower. And in bed. We should have the place to ourselves."

"I have you to myself right here. The air is warm and the rain makes the perfect music." He nuzzled his nose into the curve where her neck met her shoulder. His hands he held wrapped around her biceps. "We have everything we need."

They didn't have anything, to Sydney's way of thinking. "Do you have a condom?"

"We don't need a condom."

"What are you talking—"

"Shh. Trust me." He let her go for the length of time it took him to shuck off his shirt. Then he pulled her close again, his hands again filled with her breasts. "I want you to do something for me."

"What?" she managed, frustrated beyond words and getting more so by the minute. His hair-dusted skin tickled her back, and she snuggled up against him. Whatever he had in mind would not come close to the fun they could be having in bed.

"Take off your shorts. Your panties, too."

She pulled in a sharp breath. He wanted her naked. In the privacy of the pagoda, in the open air, in the mist from the rain…he wanted her bared to his eyes, his hands, his body.

Sydney closed her eyes, finished loosening the drawstring of the shorts and tugged them over her hips and down her legs, taking off her panties at the same time. The breeze caressed skin covered with a fine wet sheen.

She ran her hands down her face, then over her breasts and to her belly and her thighs. Then she turned to undress Ray.

He held her still, facing away. "Let me do this."

She wanted to ask him, "Do what?" but he was already taking off his shorts and then showing her, with his hands holding her hands, moving her fingers the way he wanted them to move over the length to the head of his cock. He groaned, a deep, resonant sound that sent a shiver down her spine.

Her hands were greedy, measuring his response as she stroked, using his release of clear fluid to ease the friction. Leaning back against his chest, she reached deep between his legs, taking the heavy weight of his testicles in her palms and gently caressing the pouch of tender skin. He was so incredibly soft and warm. So beautifully, utterly male.

This time when he groaned, he pulled her hands

away and drew her body flush to his. Naked skin to naked skin. And then he said, "Spread your legs."

She parted her thighs as he nudged them apart with his knee. Then he pressed forward with his body, sliding his erection between her legs. She squeezed her thighs together, trapping him there, but gently, with a grip that still allowed him to stroke.

"I need to know if you're protected from pregnancy." He moved his hands back to her belly. The heels of his palms pressed beneath her navel; his fingers delved lower to separate her folds. "I want to do this. But if there's a chance you could get pregnant, I want to make sure I don't come anywhere near you."

She shook her head. It wasn't pregnancy that concerned her. "I'm on the Pill. But—"

"I'm safe, Sydney," he said, cutting off her objection. "I do dangerous work and I'm tested regularly. The only thing you could catch from me is a baby, but I don't think either one of us is ready for that."

No. She wasn't. "What about other…"

"Other women?" he asked. He took a deep breath and let it out slowly. "I haven't been with anyone for three years. Not since the trip with Patrick."

"Ray…I…" She didn't even know what to say. He was such a physical man. How could he not—

"Shh. Don't say anything. No talking about the past, remember?" He whispered the words into her ear. "This is about now. Only now."

He was right. This was about now. This was the reason she was here. This was what she wanted. Never had she felt so safe in the arms of a man.

So she closed her eyes and let Ray have his way.

He moved his hands, sliding them between her legs and over her mound, slicking one finger through her folds while his other hand held her open, exposing her clit to the air and his touch.

And all the while he thrust, using their shared moisture to ease his way between her legs. His hand took up the same rhythm, his fingers filling her, stroking in and out, his thumb circling the hard nub where desire burned.

She couldn't take it anymore. His strong body at her back, the sound of the wind and the rain and the sea all around, his hands working sexual magic from her belly to her womb, while he made the motions of love between her thighs.

She cried out and let go. He pressed his palm hard to her mound. She shuddered, digging her fingers into his hips behind her. And he continued to stroke, to thrust, his penis sliding slickly against her skin.

His motions increased in speed and intensity. His body pumped hard and suddenly he jerked back one hand, gripping his shaft and pressing the head of his penis hard to her leg. The warmth of his release pulsed against her. And all she could do was hold him close.

DRAPING AN ARM around Sydney's shoulders, Ray headed out into the downpour. They'd waited for a little while after making love, holding one another close while they'd silently stood and waited for the storm to pass. Their breathing had settled into the same pattern, and neither one of them had felt the need to speak.

But the clouds didn't seem to have any intention

of dissipating, and Sydney was beginning to shiver. The screened walls of the pagoda were doing what they could to block the blowing rain, which was turning out to be a whole lot of nothing. Ray was just as wet now as he'd been when he'd first run under the shelter.

They needed to get back to the villa and dried off. Not to mention that it was lunchtime and Ray could eat the rump out of a rhino. Sex did that to him. Even modified sex. Add the fact that the sex was with Sydney and, well, he was starved.

He couldn't remember another completion that had been so damn satisfying and so damn scary at the same time. He wasn't sure where things between them would go from here other than to the nearest proper bed at the earliest opportunity. He wasn't going to leave here without having her all the way. And after that? Hell, he couldn't think straight until after that, so he might as well enjoy the here and now.

The rain picked up in intensity and Sydney wrapped her arms around his waist, her hands laced on his far side, her face buried close to his shoulder. God, but she was gorgeous. Yes, in her physical appearance, all long-limbed and slender, but lushly curved the way a woman should be. But it was the beauty of her inner self that had caught him off guard.

It was the way she took care of and gave so much of herself to those around her. She was making sure Chloe had the time she needed to go back to school. And Sydney never complained about Macy's monthly game nights or the meetings he'd heard the partners held at Lauren's loft. Meetings that, from what he understood, were more monkey than business.

Hell, Sydney even refused to let the housekeeper do the job she was paid to do. No, she had to be right there in the kitchen helping out while still playing hostess. He wasn't sure he'd ever known a woman more generous.

But nothing had prepared him for the way she'd come apart in his hands. He'd never doubted her passionate nature. He'd experienced her response when he'd taken her virginity. Thing was, back then he hadn't known what he'd held in his hands. All these years later and he knew. He knew.

Sydney Ford was a rare woman, complicated and complex. Which made him feel even more privileged to have been her first lover, never mind why. Whether he'd only been in the right place at the right time, or he'd been the only right one for Sydney, he'd still been lucky that she'd left that graduation party with him.

Of course he couldn't help being curious. Understanding the workings of Sydney's eighteen-year-old mind would help him better understand who she'd become. And knowing that would help him figure out the easiest way to let her go.

Because he had to let her go.

His arm tightened reflexively around her shoulders. He was having too much fun, growing too close to her, wanting more than he could possibly have. He'd realized the danger yesterday during the time they'd spent playing in the lagoon. Their fun had been natural, comfortable, incredibly sexy and a springboard to deeper, more dangerous waters.

He had to keep his focus on his work. There were no guarantees he'd walk away from his next assignment, so that ruled out making a serious commitment. He couldn't do that to a woman.

He couldn't do that to Sydney.

And only God knew where he'd find the strength to do it to himself.

7

Eight years earlier...

SYDNEY COULD NOT believe she was so clueless. So ignorant. So totally stupid and so totally lame. She'd actually thought things would be different, that graduation and the looming reality of college would've changed her classmates' mental focus. But no. Collectively they couldn't have produced one forward-thinking brain.

Half the kids in her graduating class acted as if they belonged in grade school. The rest were caught in a high-school time warp with little hope for the future. Forget maturity. Forget the idea of growing up. Forget a single one of them realizing she wasn't at all what they assumed her to be.

So what if her mother agreed and, minutes before Izzy had stopped to pick Sydney up, had even told her so to her face? What in hell did her mother know, anyway? Except how to make everyone's lives miserable, while all the time, the world revolved around her. She was flamboyant and beautiful and exciting, all the things that were out of Sydney's reach, no matter how hard she'd tried to measure up.

And now, on top of all that, Sydney was stuck here at this stupid party, with a bunch of spoiled brats.

And it was nobody's fault but her own.

Standing with her back against an eight-foot-high cedar fence, holding a plastic cup of beer she didn't even want, much less like, she remained halfway hidden in the shadow of a huge spreading oak. The night was warm and muggy. Her jeans were sticky and hot. The plastic band of her watch was causing a circle of sweat around her wrist.

Why had she ever let Izzy talk her into coming? *Because you had to get out of the house, that's why.* And she wasn't going to go home again until she'd proved every single one of her mother's accusations wrong. Considering the way things had gone in her life lately, that could take a year or two.

This party was definitely not how Sydney would choose to celebrate her graduation. Or anyone's graduation. She could be home taking a nap, for all the fun she was having. But being at home would mean another confrontation with her mother and having to hear again what a loser she was.

Of course, being a loser probably had a lot to do with why she'd rather be anywhere but here. Except for Izzy, everyone Sydney had seen here so far shared her mother's opinion. Her yearbook photo caption could've read "Coldest Fish." Instead, it didn't say anything.

She barely even knew the guys throwing the party. She thought this was Boom Daily's house, but she hadn't seen him, so she couldn't be sure. Even Izzy was uncertain. They'd just followed the crowd from the mall parking lot like the mindless lemmings they obviously were.

Stereo speakers had been moved onto the backyard

patio, where tables were set up with chips and cookies and sandwiches. Coolers of canned soft drinks sat beneath. And then there was the keg of beer at the side of the house, supplied by a group of older kids who'd been out of school long enough to be legal. And obviously feeling obligated to initiate Sydney's class into the finer things in life.

Sydney stared into her cup. How could anyone think this beer tasted like anything other than horse piss? Oh, wait. Maybe the same twenty-something bunch who thought crashing a high-school graduation bash the epitome of fun. Right. Like that would be on her "to do" list in three or four years. God, she was in a bad mood.

Slipping her arm behind the trunk of the tree, she upended her cup. The beer foamed in a puddle on the grass, soaking into the roots and the bed of purple and yellow pansies circling the trunk. Even as rotten as it was, she doubted it would do any good as a fertilizer. Maybe insecticide. Or weed killer.

"It's only free if you drink it, you know. If you dump it out, it costs you a buck."

At the sound of the deep male voice, Sydney turned her head sharply. And then she thought she was going to ooze into the ground, along with the beer. She certainly wasn't going to be able to say anything; her heart was pounding so hard she could barely breathe.

It was Ray Coffey, Patrick Coffey's older brother, the top-billed star of so many of her fantasies and daydreams, the object of the most ridiculous crush she'd ever had on a boy. The only crush she'd ever had on a boy. Except Ray Coffey barely resembled the boy she'd last seen at his graduation a year ago.

Funny how it had been only a year. He looked so much older than that. He seemed taller, though she was sure that he wasn't. Or did guys keep growing till they were twenty years old? His shoulders were definitely broader. So was his chest. As if he'd been lifting a lot of weights the past year. He probably had been, playing college football and all.

She wondered if he was still going out with Mandy Green.

"What?" he asked, his mouth breaking into the cutest dimpled grin, his eyes twinkling. "You don't like beer?"

Oh, God. She was staring at him as though he'd been speaking a foreign language. "I'm sorry, uh, yeah. I do like beer. Sometimes." Great. Now she sounded like a moron. "What I mean is, I like certain brands of beer more than others." And now she sounded like a total bitch.

"And keggo isn't one of them?"

"Keggo?" she repeated.

"Yeah. Keg o' beer."

She was still working to gather her thoughts when he grimaced and said, "That was pretty bad, wasn't it."

"Not as bad as the beer," she said, and laughed. "I'm sorry. That probably makes me sound like a snob. And I don't mean to be. I mean, I'm not, really."

"It's okay. I'm not much for keggo beer myself," he said, and handed her the cold Corona long-neck he'd had stuck in the pocket of his jeans. "Better?"

"This will definitely do," she said, and twisting off the top, took a long appreciative swallow. Appreciative that he apparently wasn't going to hold her snobbery against her and appreciative of the better-tasting beer.

That was what she got for having had only the better brands to filch from the family fridge.

"Now that's my kind of woman." Ray laughed. "One who can go for a good beer, instead of wanting one of those silly frou-frou drinks."

God, she loved the way he laughed. The sound of it. The look on his face. The way her belly got all warm and tight and tingly. "I should warn you, then. I'm a big fan of those silly frou-frou drinks."

He tipped his long-neck bottle toward her. "Well, never let it be said that I let a strawberry daiquiri come between me and a good time."

Was he having a good time? With her? Sydney felt about thirteen years old. And she was afraid that if she wasn't careful, Ray would discover that she had this *huge* crush on him.

But it was hard to play it cool when he was here and he was talking to her, not to any of the guys he knew and not to any of the girls whom she'd heard in the past say they'd drop their pants if he asked.

"I'm Ray Coffey, by the way. Patrick's brother." He took a drink of his beer.

"Oh, hi. I'm Sydney Ford."

"Yeah. I knew that."

Oh, God. He knew who she was! "I knew who you were, too."

"Well, that's cool. That we know each other and all." He shrugged. "I always have to remind myself that not everyone I went to school with knows who I am."

"I think most people you went to school with know. You were rather high-profile." Sydney cocked her head to one side, hoping it made her look cute rather than stupid. She was not much good at flirting. "Let's see. There was football and the class-president thing and the school paper. And weren't you crowned five or six different kinds of king?"

Ray smacked his palm to his forehead. "That's right. I'm royalty. Well, retired royalty, anyway."

"Does that mean I should curtsy?" she asked, doing her best not to fall at his feet.

"If you do, then I'll have to bow." He stared at her over his bottle of beer as he drank.

"Bow?" Sydney frowned, but only as long as it took her to snap to what he was saying. And then she chuckled. She couldn't help it. He had no idea what sort of crap he'd just stepped into. Especially tonight.

"The Ice Queen thing, right?" She rolled her eyes, shook her head. "I'm really not, you know. It's just one of those bad rumors that won't go away."

Ray took a step closer, reached out a hand and lightly tugged on a strand of her hair where it skimmed her shoulder. "So how'd the rumor get started?"

She shrugged, sipped from the bottle of beer. He'd touched her hair and she wasn't sure she could answer his question without her voice cracking.

And she so wished she'd worn a tank top or spaghetti straps so she could've felt his touch on her skin. Instead, she was wearing this stupid Depeche Mode concert T-shirt she'd grabbed when Izzy had honked, figuring they were only going to the mall.

"I'm really not sure."

"Hmm." Ray looked at her. "The way I figure, it could be any number of things."

He was nice to try to be so diplomatic, but she really did know the truth, even if she'd lied to him about it. "What number of things?"

"You've got that blond-hair-and-blue-eyes thing going on. Sort of an icy Scandinavian look."

"And I think we both know that's a load of BS," she said, though she couldn't deny a small thrill that he'd noticed her looks.

"Well, then," he said, grinning again, leaning back against the fence almost right behind where she stood in the shadows of the tree. "I guess it's just because you're so cool."

She braced a shoulder on the tree trunk and studied his face. If only being "cool" was anywhere close to the truth. He had to know what everyone thought. If he knew who she was, there was no way he couldn't know what everyone thought. She wondered then if he was just playing with her, getting her hopes up before he crushed her to the ground.

But that didn't seem to fit with the kind of guy she knew he was. And so she decided to be totally honest. She could only hope he wouldn't walk away. "You're close. You just need to drop the temperature a few more degrees."

Sydney said what she had to say, then waited. The party was getting louder, the music and the people. The laughter was nothing but screeching and now a dozen of the kids were splashing in the Dailys' backyard pool.

She wanted nothing more than to be somewhere else right now. It wasn't the crowd. It wasn't even the kids making up the crowd. Yes, they were getting on her nerves, but after four years she really was used to their antics.

No, her bad mood was all about the things her mother had said. The accusations she'd made and the names she'd called her. Sydney guessed her mother was including her, along with her father, in the divorce.

"Listen," Ray finally said. "I need to get another beer."

Sydney's heart fell to her stomach and both made the trip to her feet. Pretty much what she'd expected. "Sure. Go ahead."

"No." He shook his head, grinned, lifted his empty bottle. "Let me try that again. The rest of this six-pack's in my truck. You want to come with me?"

RAY HAD NEVER had to work at being popular. He'd never really cared about being popular. It all just sort of happened because of the things he'd done in school. And, okay. He supposed girls thought he was cute. But he didn't have anything to do with that.

He remembered having wondered a lot about Sydney Ford during his senior year. Patrick hadn't known much about her except that everyone called her a cold fish. When Ray had asked his brother why, Patrick had shrugged and headed out the door to shoot hoops, which was all he ever wanted to do.

For some reason, ever since Ray had seen Sydney Ford standing in the doorway of the computer lab last year, he'd had a hard time getting her out of his mind. And he wasn't sure why. He'd been dating Mandy

Green, so he'd never really done anything about figuring it out.

But the minute he'd walked into Boom Daily's backyard, looking for the guys he'd played football with, he'd seen her standing in the corner between the fence and the tree and he knew the time had come to make his move. There was nothing he loved more than a good challenge, and he'd learned a thing or two about making moves this past year at A&M.

Sticking that extra long-neck bottle in his pocket had been a stroke of genius. He'd had a feeling Sydney Ford would've been used to a better class of beer than what these cheapskates had sprung for. She had a bad rep for being a snob. He'd just never seen anything to back it up.

Maybe it was because he'd worked with Isabel Leighton on the school paper. He knew Izzy and trusted her judgment. She didn't put up with bullshit. And she was Sydney's best friend. That was enough to make Ray wonder. To make him want to discover the truth about Sydney Ford for himself—and only slightly less than he wanted to get her clothes off and get his hands on her body. For a cold fish, she was the hottest thing going in *his* book.

They'd just reached his pickup parked against the curb half a block away when he heard sirens. He had a bad feeling about this. A really bad feeling. He looked from the beer cooler in the truck bed to Sydney and took a chance. "You want to get outta here?"

Her expression was a sort of dazed confusion. She frowned and she blinked and she said, "I thought you wanted to party."

He was thinking of a more private party, but he was really thinking that it wasn't going to be a good thing for Sydney to get busted for drinking underage. He jerked his head toward the sound of sirens, getting closer.

"I think it might be a good idea if we leave before either of us gets invited to take another kind of ride."

Her eyes widened, and when he opened the driver's-side door, she hopped in and slid across the bench seat. He followed and managed to get the keys out of his pocket, into the ignition and pull away from the curb before the red, white and blue lights flashed in his rearview mirror.

When they reached the stop sign at the end of the street, he blew out a breath and cast a quick glance at Sydney. "That was a little too close."

Her face remained impassive, but he caught a hint of emotion in her voice when she said, "Wouldn't that have given my mother a shock and a half. Her only daughter arrested!"

"Yeah, and then you'd have to go through alcohol-awareness classes and community service, and it's all such a pain in the ass. This way you're saved the trouble and don't have to get bitched out by your mom."

Sydney lifted her chin and gave a sharp huff. "I think mine would've congratulated me for having the balls to break the law. It would give her hope that I don't really have a stick up my ass."

What the hell? Ray looked over. "Your mother told you you have a stick up your ass?"

"Never mind." She waved off his question, then waited a minute and, crossing one leg beneath her on the seat, turned toward him and asked, "Where are we going?"

Ray had returned his gaze to the street ahead so he couldn't be sure, but he swore Sydney had just scooted closer. "Actually, I'm just driving. Getting us outta there. You have anyplace you want to go?"

She thought for a minute while he pulled out of the gated subdivision. "What about the water wall?"

They weren't too far away. Sure. Why the hell not? Ray headed for the man-made waterfall at the Transco Fountain in the Galleria. He'd noticed Sydney's T-shirt earlier so he flipped down his visor and grabbed his Depeche Mode *Violator* CD. Though she kept her voice low, he could hear her as she sang along with "Personal Jesus." And she had a good voice.

She also had a most excellent body, which for some reason she couldn't keep still. She was doing a whole lot of shifting about on the truck seat while he drove and she sang and the music played. They didn't talk, and she didn't ask if he minded, but halfway through the next song she did a fast-forward to find "Policy of Truth" before sitting back dead center in the seat.

Ray nearly groaned. Another six inches and she'd be in his lap. She'd been working her way there for the past ten minutes. And she had to be doing it on purpose. He wondered if he should pull her on over, and he went so far as to lay his arm along the back of the seat. She leaned back and her hair brushed his arm and he almost dropped his hand to her shoulder, but he'd waited too long. They were there.

He parked around the block, behind the adjacent lawn, figuring the short walk through the landscaped park would be a good time to talk. He'd wanted to get to know her for a long time now, and she obviously wanted to get to know him. He didn't want to screw this up.

She turned toward him and moved closer, easing her way the rest of the distance between them. Their thighs brushed. He reached for his door handle, ready to let both of them out the truck. Sydney leaned across his body and wrapped her fingers around his hand, holding him still, catching her bottom lip with her teeth, looking up from beneath her long lashes with eyes that belonged in a bedroom.

"I thought you wanted to party," she said, and Ray's hard-on answered for him. He couldn't believe this was happening.

He let go of the door but not of her hand. He did shift his butt enough to lean back in the corner where the seat met the door. He used his eyes to invite her to come over. She stared at him for what seemed like an eternity, and her eyes were so bright and so blue.

Then she smiled, and Ray was afraid his dick was going to explode when she braced her hand high on his thigh and leaned forward. He didn't even hesitate. He dropped his arm to her back and hauled her as close as he could. Her mouth was already opened when he touched it with his, so he gave her what she seemed to want.

And she gave it to him right back. Mandy Green had never kissed him like this. The girls at A&M who'd taken him on as their pet sex project had come close, but no cigar. Because this kiss was as real as it got. For some reason Sydney Ford wanted him in ways he'd only imagined. She was telling him so with her mouth. And with the hand making its way to his fly.

He knew he was being stupid, but he didn't give a shit. He let her touch him. He helped her touch him, pressing down on her hand where he needed her to press, cupping her fingers the way he needed her fingers cupped. He ground himself into her hand and he shuddered and then he stopped. He wanted to get his hands on her.

He tried, but their position was awkward and he couldn't find the hem of her T-shirt without pushing her away. And he sure didn't want her going anywhere, not when she had such a warm and willing mouth. But then she pulled back. And, as he watched, she touched her fingers to her mouth, spreading the wetness from their kiss into her bottom lip. And then she totally blew him away.

"Could we get a room?"

"Uh, okay." God, he was going to come in his pants. "If that's what you want."

She nodded. "That's what I want."

Keeping his arm around Sydney's shoulders, Ray used his left hand to turn the key in the ignition and pull away from the curb. He wasn't a virgin, but he was pretty inexperienced when it came to renting a room. Most of his encounters had been in dorm rooms or frat houses or back seats of cars.

He had money. He had condoms. He had Sydney and a hard-on that could break bricks. The only problem he could think of was patience. He didn't have any. And nerves. He had too many of those.

What in the hell was going on here? He was about to take the Ice Queen to bed. That was what.

OH, GOD. WHAT WAS she doing here? Alone with Ray Coffey, sitting in the front seat of his truck while he rented a motel room. With a bed. She couldn't believe she was doing this and released a short burst of laughter.

She sounded hysterical. Her teeth were chattering. She was going to lose her virginity with Ray. The only boy she'd ever wanted to sleep with. Except he was no longer a boy.

She watched him as he returned from the motel office, his hands stuffed into the pockets of his jeans. As if he was hiding the key to the room. As if he didn't want anyone to see. Sydney closed her eyes.

She was being ridiculous. Silly, immature and ridiculous. Traits that were obviously the truth or her own mother wouldn't have called her on them and encouraged her to loosen up and enjoy life.

To get the stick out of her ass.

To get laid.

She wondered if Mandy Green's mother had told her to get laid. If Mandy Green had had sex with Ray Coffey. And if there was any way at all Sydney could show him a good time when she didn't have a clue what to do. Okay. She'd read enough of *Cosmo* to know the mechanics. She'd even read an article somewhere called ''The Gentle Taking of Virginity.'' But with the way her stomach was about to heave, she didn't know how she was supposed to relax. Much less enjoy.

The truck door swung open. Sydney blinked as Ray climbed into the cab. He was quiet as he drove down the length of the two-story structure, reading the room numbers until he found the one he was looking for.

He parked. He got out. He held the door as she climbed down. He placed his hand in the small of her back and guided her toward the right.

And then they were there. He turned the key and Sydney stepped inside and he followed and pushed the door closed.

The snap of the lock nearly did her in.

She started to shake. Her stomach rolled queasily. The room was dark, the only light a sliver thrown across the two double beds from the slit where the drawn drapes didn't quite meet. She'd just decided to make a run for the bathroom when she felt Ray's hands on her shoulders, his lips teasing her ear where she'd nervously tucked her hair behind.

She lifted her chin as the tremors making her so nervous settled in the pit of her belly. And lower, between her legs, where she felt herself grow damp. She'd had these feelings before, lying in bed, dreaming, wondering, waking from a deep sleep and thinking of Ray.

But he was here and this was real. She was responding to him, to the touch of his lips, *his* hands and not the touch of her own beneath the bedcovers. Nerves became desire and she couldn't wait to feel him. So when he reached for the hem of her T-shirt, she lifted her arms.

The room's refrigerated air chilled her skin and she shivered, but Ray was warm and solid and reassuring at her back. She turned in his arms and silently thanked him for leaving the light off. Later she wanted to see his face. Right now she was afraid she was going to cry. She might not be sexually experienced, but she knew enough to be pretty damn sure tears were not a turn-on.

Praying for capable and not clumsy fingers, she reached for the buttons at the neckline of the maroon-and-white Aggies' pullover he wore. But when she went to tug the shirt from the waistband of his jeans, he stopped her.

"Sydney, wait."

She froze. "What's wrong?"

"Nothing's wrong. As far as I'm concerned, everything's right."

"Why did you stop me?"

"Are you sure about this? Really sure?"

He sounded as if he was the one who wasn't sure. "I'm here, aren't I?"

"Yeah. You are." He let go of her hands and moved his fingers to the straps of her bra. "But for the life of me I can't figure out why."

His hands were shaking. Sydney closed her eyes and wrapped her fingers in the material of his shirt. What was she supposed to tell him?

That a girl had to lose her virginity sooner or later? That she was being a dutiful daughter and doing exactly what her mother had told her to do? That she'd had a crush on him forever and she wanted him, more than anyone, to know that she wasn't a cold fish?

Finally she leaned forward and, through the V at his neckline kissed the warm skin of his chest. "I'm here because I want to be with you. Isn't that enough?"

At her whispered answer, he gripped her shoulders and blew out a steadying breath. She felt his rapid heartbeat where she'd pressed her forehead to his

chest, felt his shaking fingers where they pulled her
straps down her shoulders. She lifted her head and
looked up through the shadows in time to catch his
descending mouth.

His kiss was gentle. He was seducing her with his
lips and his tongue even while his hands moved to
the catch on the back of her bra and set her loose.
Stepping back, he put enough distance between them
for her to slip her arms free. When he attempted to
take back her mouth, she shook her head, insisting he
allow her to finish what she'd tried to start. She
tugged his shirt up and over his head.

When he wrapped her in his arms and pulled her
close, she thought she was going to die. She'd never
imagined anything, anyone…no, she'd never imagined Ray feeling this good. The muscles in his back
were solid and hard, the muscles in his chest the
same. The hair there tickled her breasts and her nose
when she nuzzled close. He smelled wonderful. Clean
and amazingly sweet. And his hands at her back made
her feel as if she was the tiniest little thing.

He backed up toward the bed, taking her with him.
He sat, holding her by the waist. His thumbs met in
the center of her belly. Her eyes had adjusted to the
room's dim light, and she was able to see more now
than she had been. Which meant Ray was probably
also better able to see. And he was looking at her
breasts, which she wished were a cup size larger.

Slowly, gently, he skated his palms up her rib cage
until he was able to stroke both her nipples with his
thumbs. Sydney tossed her head back and held tight
to his forearms. Her body trembled and she hated for
him to think she was frightened. She was…in a good

way and of what was to come. But not of him. Never of him.

When he pulled her closer and lowered his head, when he took a nipple into his mouth, she could hardly keep from crying out. His tongue, oh, his tongue. So warm and so wet. Rasping over her sensitive skin so that her nipples drew into hard swollen peaks. And then he trailed his kisses down her belly, licking at her belly button while sliding his hands down her sides…to the brass button of her jeans.

He lifted his head, released the button, took the zipper all the way down. Oh, God, had she shaved her legs? Yes. What panties was she wearing? She thought back to getting dressed. Cotton, bikinis. Plain pink, she thought, yes, to match her pink lace bra.

And then she couldn't think anymore because Ray's thumbs were tucked beneath her waistband and he was tugging the denim over her hips. She shimmied to help and heel-toed off her black Nikes. While she did that, he leaned back and lifted one leg, then the other, to tug off his boots.

Sydney kicked her jeans free and stood wearing only the barest scrap of pink. But when Ray reached out to pull her panties down, she stopped him, holding his hands in place at her hips. "Not yet."

She swore she heard a strangled groan when he said, "You've changed your mind."

He was so amazingly cute. And so nice to actually be willing to stop. Instinct told her how revealing that was, how rare and how special. She was afraid what she had on him was not a crush at all. A crush seemed way too simple for the flutters and the hope she was feeling.

"I haven't changed my mind. I just want you to take your pants off."

He laughed then, and she didn't think she'd ever seen anyone get out of a pair of jeans so fast. And then they were standing in the dark room in only their socks and their underwear. The cold fish and the boy she was afraid was going to make her fall in love.

When he pulled her into his arms, she went willingly, savoring the warmth of his skin and his much larger body and the press of his erection so hard against her giving flesh.

When he tugged her down to the bed, she followed without hesitation, loving the way their legs tangled together, the way his hands seemed to be everywhere at once, the time he took with his kisses before stripping them both of the rest of their clothes.

When he moved to cover her with his body, she welcomed him with a joy she hadn't known existed, with all the warmth she had to offer, with silent tears that told her she'd never done anything so right.

8

"CAN YOU BELIEVE this?" Hands in the pockets of his khaki fatigues, Anton shook his head as he took in the ancient temples surrounding the two plazas of which the archaeological site was comprised. "Two thousand years and so much of it is still here. The materials, the workmanship. It's absolutely amazing."

Standing beside Anton at the Mayan ruins of Altun Ha, Lauren found herself equally awed—but awed by the man at her side. His passion for his profession was evident in so many of his endeavors, but was especially palpable here and now, witnessing similar labors undertaken by some of the world's earliest architects.

She knew he didn't recognize the extent of his passion even as she knew his inner fire played a big part in the attraction that continued to draw them together. That fire was her perfect complement, emotional, as well as sexual, yet for some reason, in both arenas, he held his deepest self in check.

She wanted to knock that self-control into another dimension, she thought, smiling indulgently. More than anything, she wanted to make him let go. Selfish of her, she supposed, wanting to be there, wanting the experience, wanting to feel what happened when he finally did.

Of course *he* didn't think he was overly controlling, just as she didn't think she was overly sexed. A typical relationship tit for tat, she supposed. Though they weren't going to have a romance to tit or to tat if they didn't work on finding a solution, a compromise, or both.

Which meant they each had to face the other's criticism with an open mind.

Lauren wasn't sure that was possible.

They'd rented an old Jeep in Belize City and had spent the morning navigating the narrow winding road to the area's most extensively excavated Mayan site. The ruins were a big part of the Central American country's attraction, and organized tours were regularly scheduled.

Anton, however, had insisted they set their own timetable. He didn't want to be rushed. He wanted to see the sites in his own time and his own way. Lauren could hardly object. The privacy was something they needed.

"Did you always want to be an architect?" She glanced from the man back to the sixty-foot-high ruin. During their too-short time living together, he'd told her about his studies, his internship, the struggles of establishing the firm with Doug. But he'd never shared the beginnings of his dream. She wondered if she hadn't invited the confidence, or if he'd thought she wouldn't care.

A smile brightened Anton's face, softening his features, erasing so many of the lines and reminding Lauren of the face she'd fallen in love with, a face that seemed to have lost the ability to smile. She was glad to see she was wrong—even though he hadn't smiled for her.

"Only since I was about four or five and had enough Legos to build barracks for all my G.I. Joes." The corner of his mouth quirked up farther, but after a moment spent in private thought, he reset his mouth into an unyielding line.

Lauren found that she'd balled her hands into fists deep in her pockets and had to force herself to relax. As Anton started walking toward the Jeep, she followed, casting a quick look up at the darkening sky after a drop of rain splashed against her cheek. "I don't think you ever told me that. About the Legos and G.I. Joes."

"There are a lot of things I've never told you." He tossed the comment at her defensively almost, as if he'd taken her remark as an accusation. "Things that never came up in conversation. It's not like I've been hiding anything."

Lauren ground her teeth. At times she really felt as though she couldn't win for losing. "I didn't mean to imply that you had. What I meant is that it's fun to hear that type of thing about you. I don't know if I've ever thought of you as a little boy with building blocks before."

She visually measured the breadth of his shoulders as he led her from the plaza. "I'll bet you were cute."

Anton stopped walking, turned and glanced back as if wondering what it was she had on her mind. He frowned, but his mouth did break into a grin. This time, a grin meant for her.

"Cute as a bug in a rug, or so I was told over and over and over and over," he said, rolling his eyes.

Lauren grinned back. "With big blond curls?"

He shook his head so that the curls bounced. "Even bigger and blonder than the ones I have now. Pretty damn sissy-looking, if you want to know the truth."

Maybe then. Now he was anything but, with his chiseled features and the everyday stubble that followed the line of his jaw and chin. Lauren knew intimately the texture of his sexy, barely there beard. As well as the feel of his hair as her fingers slid through it.

She suppressed a rising shiver. "In all the time I spent at your parents' place, I don't think I saw any pictures of you as a kid. They were all more recent."

He looked at her for a long moment, blinking slowly, though his frown never fully returned. "Where are you going with this, Lauren?"

Hands in the pockets of her cotton walking shorts, she shrugged. "I don't know that I'm going anywhere. I was just realizing how many things about you I don't know. And I'm sorry I never got to know you better when I had the chance."

"I didn't exactly make it easy for you." He looked toward the sky, looked back again with an expression of regret. "I can be pretty single-minded."

"Is that the same as hardheaded?" she teased, hoping to dispel what she was afraid was his impending acceptance that things between them were over. She didn't want them to be over. Not yet. Not this way.

"You're cute, you know that?" He tugged on a lock of her hair, tucked it behind her ear. His touch lingered, slowly caressing. Then with his gaze holding hers, he trailed the back of his fingers the length of her neck.

Lauren closed her eyes and shuddered. God, she had missed his touch. True, they'd slept close together the other night, and that casual connection had given her a sense of security, a grounding she desperately needed.

But it was nothing compared to this simple touch, a touch that to Lauren's mind defined the intimacy she'd been missing.

So when Anton suddenly pulled away, she looked up.

His expression appeared to be a strange mix of sadness and confusion. "Why do you do that?"

"Do what?" she asked, and frowned. Why did she react to his touch? Was that what he was asking? How could he not understand? Especially after all this time? "Why do I enjoy the way your hands make me feel? Is that what you want to know? Do you think I shouldn't enjoy the way you touch me?"

"No, I'm not saying that at all. I'd be surprised if you didn't enjoy having me touch you," he added, lifting a sardonic brow. "You've told me more than a few times how you feel about sex, and I certainly have enough experience to draw on."

"Why is my sexuality such a problem for you?" When he didn't answer, Lauren hung her head. Then she looked back. And then she looked away. "I never understood why my getting into our physical relationship made you so uncomfortable. It was like you held back."

This was what she hated to ask, but what, more

than anything, she needed to know. "Did you? Hold back? Because of me?"

He all but shuffled his feet. "What do you want me to say, Lauren? Do you really want me to be honest? Okay, then. Here's your honesty. I held back because I didn't know if what you were feeling was real. If you were real. If you were feeling for me, because of me...with me. Or if you were just...feeling. For the sake of feeling."

Of course sex was about physical feeling. But that was not all it was and Anton knew that. He had to know that. He couldn't really believe she hadn't involved her emotions. Not after all this time.

Rain began to fall steadily, but Lauren didn't care. "I'm not about to deny that I love sex. And I'm not going to deny myself that enjoyment. But it's being with the person you love...it's me being with you that makes it work. That makes it good. I can't believe you don't know that."

He didn't answer. Not with spoken words or with body language or with an expression she was able to read. The only thing he did was grab her hand and pull. "Let's get out of the rain. Then we can talk."

Her preference would have been to stand in the rain and let the water wash away her building disappointment. She *so* did not want to get into a fight. Not after the way things had been going so beautifully between them the past several days.

But Anton's hand and pace were both insistent and so she set off at a brisk jog behind him. They reached the parked Jeep just as the first cloud burst. And between fumbling with the keys and struggling with the doors, both were more than a little wet by the time they climbed inside.

Lauren was glad she'd put her hair in a braid. She slicked her palms up her forehead before the water beaded there ran into her eyes. She shook off her arms and, with nowhere to wipe her hands, finally settled on her cotton tank top, which was a wasted effort because the material had absorbed all the water it was going to absorb.

The emotional overload hit her and she looked up and laughed. She laughed until she saw the fire burning in Anton's eyes, and then her giggles died in her belly, replaced by an anticipation she hadn't felt for what seemed like ages. Like forever. Since the day she'd walked away and left him swimming laps in his pool.

The heat was one that came from a place deep inside him, a place he'd rarely shared. It was the fire she longed to see, a fire burning for her. The emotion she'd so seldom been able to tap when she'd nearly broken her heart trying. Hope flared, along with desire.

She remained sitting sideways in her seat, one leg crooked beneath her, the other on the floor, and dropped her hands to her thighs, where her fingers squeezed. She did her best to keep her expression and her tone level when what she felt was upside down. "What is it? What's wrong?"

Slowly he took a deep breath, released it with a muttered curse, then looked away. "You make it hard."

"Make what hard?"

"Saying no. Staying away." He turned back to her

again. His expression had softened but desire still reigned. "I don't think you have any idea how sexy you are. The things that come to mind when I look at you. The things I want to do. It's crazy. Nothing else…" He shook his head. "No one else has ever gotten to me the way you have. The way you do."

Not the words of a man in love, were they? For a moment all Lauren could do was sit and stare and try to get past the hurt of what he hadn't said. Humidity and confusion enveloped her, and perspiration replaced the drops of rain on her skin. Thoughts raced through her mind, leaving her to think that this wasn't about her, after all.

Maybe he wasn't battling demons of her making but demons of his own. Maybe he couldn't trust where her passion, her love, were coming from, what she made him feel, because that trust would mean betraying the truths he believed about himself. Just as denying her sexuality would be her own self-directed lie.

What was it he believed about himself that kept him at such a distance? And how in the world were they going to find a middle ground?

Before she could think of where to begin looking, Anton reached out and touched her, running fingertips over one breast, then the other, brushing one nipple, then the other, both well delineated by the wet cotton fabric of her top.

Of all the times to go braless, she thought, doing her damnedest to keep her face passive, her breathing even, her heartbeat from running away.

The one thing over which she had no control, the one reaction that would show Anton exactly what he was doing to her, was also the most obvious to a visually oriented man. And so he continued his caress until her nipples drew into tight gumdrops and she would've done anything to have him taste her candy.

She wanted desperately to reach for the hem of her tank top, to pull the thin fabric over her head and off, to bare her body for his enjoyment, one in which she would share. But she didn't. She sat still. And instead of closing her eyes and giving the experience over to the rest of her senses, she forced herself to keep her gaze trained on his face.

He held the weight of her breast in his palm. Tension showed in the set of his mouth, in the tic of his pulse at his temple. He looked up…from beneath his downcast brow, he looked up. The angle gave him the appearance of great impatience, gave Lauren the sense that he was losing the battle of restraint.

"Take it off."

Three simple words, and her hands started to shake. Yet, more than the words, it was the tone of voice, husky, raspy and rattled. As if he no longer had control over a thing so simple as the sound that rolled from his throat. What had been anticipation slipped quickly into anxiety, apprehension even, as she reached for the hem of the shirt. She'd never felt more vulnerable.

While she pulled it up and over her head, Anton moved his seat, sliding it all the way back and away from the steering wheel. He leaned across the console then, reaching for and releasing the lever beneath hers. Her seat shot back and bounced against its mooring. As Anton climbed across the console, his expression intent on having his way, Lauren scooted over to give him more room. The door handle jabbed mercilessly into her hip until, hands at her waist, he lifted her onto his lap. Facing him, she straddled his thighs, her knees barely fitting around his hips on the narrow seat.

He closed his eyes, shook his head and shuddered. Lauren felt the tremors in his body, his powerful attempt to hold himself in check. Powerful, but unsuccessful, because when he once again met her gaze, the expression on his face told her things he'd never said with words, things he'd rarely said with his body.

A fiercely turbulent emotion sizzled between them, and now there was no going back. She didn't want to go back. She wanted to give this man all she was. She wanted to convince him how good they were together and how far they could go when their two became one.

"What do you want me to do?" she asked even as his hands went to the fly of his fatigues. The zipper's metal teeth grated all the way down, and Lauren trembled.

She raised herself on her knees and leaned toward him. He took her breast into his mouth as she worked her shorts over her hips and off one leg, settling back onto his lap even as he raised his lower body and tugged his pants to his thighs.

His erection pressed hard against her bare sex and bare belly. Her dampness spread and she whimpered as he moved his mouth across her chest, dragging the flat of his tongue from one mound of flesh to the other, drawing hard on her nipple even as he wrapped one hand around her back and worked his fingers down to squeeze her bottom.

His other hand he wrapped around his cock. Lauren could feel his fingers there as he held himself, squeezing the base of his shaft. She couldn't believe he was already so close to coming, but the physical evidence, the bulge of flesh pulsing told a truth he couldn't deny.

His excitement heightened all that she was feeling. She looked down, seeing the hair-dusted flat of his belly beneath the rucked-up hem of his tobacco-colored T-shirt, his abs crunched and his fist pushed down into the nest of dark blond hair. His penis was beautiful, rigid and ripe, plum red and swollen. She wanted to take him in her mouth.

But their close quarters restricted movement and so, instead, she leaned back, bracing her elbows on the dashboard. Anton rubbed the head of his penis between her folds, both of them hissing in a breath at the contact, both of them watching the sex play between their legs.

She wanted to take him deep inside. Instead, she let him explore, separating her with his fingers, rubbing his penis over the tight knot of her clit, spreading her open and pushing forward and upward, inserting a crooked finger and finding her G-spot. She squirmed in his lap, especially when his finger delved deeper between her legs.

She pulled in a sharp breath at the invasion, forcing herself not to grind down into his hand. Not yet. She couldn't come yet. Not when the sight of his erection was taking her arousal to incredible heights. She had never in her life wanted to get off as badly as she did right now, in this steam pit of a car, with the man she loved making her body weep with want.

With her legs spread wide, she dropped her head back until she hit the windshield glass. Anton teased her, with his thumb and his finger and his penis, pulling the latter through her slick folds and back, over and over, back and forth.

She couldn't help it. She began to writhe, to grind her hips in a circular motion, to pump up and down. She began to pant, steaming the already steamy air. She began to come, and she stopped herself, with shudders that racked her body. And then she lifted her head.

Anton's face was flushed, his hair in ringlets falling over his forehead, his mouth a tight line and his eyes on fire. His voice came from the pit of his soul when he whispered, "Yes?"

"Oh, God, yes!" She cried out as he entered her in one long, smooth stroke. He'd been gone so long and she'd missed him so much and she'd wanted him like this forever.

She came apart, rocked from her toes to the roots of her hair. She shuddered and she shook and she shivered, sliding her fingers down into her sex and squeezing hard before rejoicing in the tactile proof of their bodies joining.

She loved touching Anton where he filled her with his penis. She looked at his face and she smiled. His head was thrown back, the tendons in his neck standing in rigid relief. He grimaced, his eyes squeezed tightly shut, his mouth open as he blew out short choppy breaths.

And then he surged upward, crying out as he filled her with the warmth of his seed. She pulled him in as deeply as their awkward position allowed, pushing him to reach for more.

A quiver throbbed the length of his body and he finally shook it off, finished and completely spent. His eyes were closed, his head back against the seat. Lauren waited, holding him deep inside, hating to let him go. Leaning forward, needing to feel the emotional connection stirred by their physical joining, she brushed his lips with hers.

He kissed her back, briefly, lightly, a token gesture of affection that had nothing to do with the heights they'd just reached with their bodies. She tried again, sweetly sucking his lower lip. He let her continue the kiss, let her tease him with the tip of her tongue, the gentle edge of her teeth.

But somewhere between one breath and the next, she was the only one involved in the mouth-to-mouth contact. Anton had retreated. And so Lauren sat up, lifting her hips to release him, tamping down the urge to cry the minute he pulled free. This wasn't how this was supposed to end.

He repaired his clothing, adjusted his still-hard penis inside his fatigues. And then he opened the passenger-side door and climbed from the Jeep. She had more to repair and adjust, but managed by the time he'd walked around to the driver's side and slid behind the wheel.

He turned on the ignition, stared out the windshield as he asked, "You are still on the Pill, right?"

A little late for that, wasn't it? "Yes. Don't worry. You won't be hearing the pitter patter of little feet nine months from now."

"Good."

The word punched her square in the stomach, making her want to curl over and retch.

He shifted into first, let off the clutch, and the Jeep jerked from the cutaway back onto the main road. Anton had nothing else to say. He made the drive back to Belize City in silence, inside a Jeep that smelled of sex.

Lauren stared out the partially opened window, welcoming the blowing rush of rain in her face. The fresh air was easier to breathe than the scent of desire gone wrong. The stinging drops pelting her skin were easier to withstand than the pain stabbing dagger-sharp in her belly.

The rain forest they passed was easier to look at than the man at her side, who no longer had a heart.

"OKAY. I HAVE a question."

Having barely recovered from yesterday's rainy-day encounter with Ray, the next afternoon found Sydney sitting on the sundeck on the roof of the villa. She glanced from Kinsey, who sat in the twin to Sydney's own fan-back chair, to Poe, who relaxed in a matching cedar lounger, to Lauren, who did not relax where she sat in hers.

Stereo speakers wired to the deck from the villa's main room played a recording of a local reggae band. The umbrella table was pulled close into the circle of the female four and loaded down with pineapple and starfruit, figs and mangoes, plums and tangerines, all which Auralie had picked up on the mainland.

The men had gone fishing. And the women had joked all afternoon about keeping the cave warm while the cavemen were out spearing dinner. Except

Lauren, who had wanted to spear Anton, a spearing of a sort that was not a sexual metaphor and was also not a joke.

Actually the women were starving and waiting, fingers crossed, for the fresh fish that Auralie had promised to bake with bananas and limes and an incredibly spicy rice pilaf for dinner. Until then, the fruit—much of it rum-soaked at Lauren's insistence—would have to do. Washing it down with the leftover rum and a wee bit of Coke meant any inhibitions they'd brought to the deck had long since met an untimely fate.

Stretching out her legs and wiggling her toes as she reached for a fig, Kinsey shot a sideways glance at Sydney. "Are you going to ask us your question, or are we supposed to snatch random answers out of the air?"

Sydney wished she was facing all three of the others. She wanted them lined up, side by side, one, two, three, so she could get a look at their expressions when she dropped her bomb.

As it was, she finished off a chunk of pineapple, licked her fingers clean, then shifted around to sit on one hip, making eye contact with each woman before asking, "Is there anyone here who hasn't had sex?"

A moment of silence. And then...

"You mean in our entire lives?" Kinsey asked, innocently disfiguring her fig. "Or while here on the island?"

There was one in every bunch. "While here on the island, smarty-pants."

Lauren frowned, bypassing the fruit she'd leaned forward to inspect and pouring herself another rum and Coke. "What kind of nosy question is that?"

Make that two smarty-pants. "What do you mean, what kind of nosy question? How many kinds of nosy questions are there? It's just nosy."

"You need to be more specific," Poe stated.

Two smarty-pants and now a troublemaker. "How can I possibly be more specific?"

"What, exactly, qualifies as sex?" Poe asked, intently considering the tines of the fork she held. "Are you specifically asking about intercourse? Or do you want to know about *any* bodily encounter? Say, kissing. Or grabbing hold of a tight male ass. And—" she pointed the fork toward Sydney "—why do you want to know?"

"As far as what qualifies as sex…" Sydney arched a brow, narrowed an eye. She should've known this wouldn't be easy. Especially with the fuzzy state of all of their brains. "I vote for any bodily encounter." She had to. What she and Ray had done in the pagoda definitely counted as sex. And, oh, what sex it had been!

"As for the why, well—" again she glanced at each of her friends "—I know one of you is having sex because I heard you. And it's been driving me crazy trying to figure out who it was. I don't know any of you the way I would need to know you to recognize your more, uh, intimate…giggles."

Spearing a tangerine wedge with her fork, Poe turned her gaze on Sydney. "You don't know any of us biblically, you mean."

As Poe poked the tangerine into her mouth, Lauren snorted. Then Kinsey giggled. Poe tried, but the sound was more of a throaty laugh.

What a bunch of goobers! Sydney shook her head.

"Pitiful, all of you. Pitiful and not even close. Try again. This time forget being silly. And you forget being such a putz," she said to Lauren. "All of you, try to imagine yourself in the throes of wild hedonistic passion. Maybe I can figure it out."

Kinsey huffed, Lauren puffed, Poe blew the house down. All four women dissolved into hysterics.

"Maybe it was a guy you heard giggling. Have you ever thought of that?"

Sydney stopped to consider Kinsey's question and considered, too, the type of sound Ray made. He rarely made any. He came silently. As if it was important, he didn't reveal a hint of vulnerability. She frowned and wondered why she'd never realized that before.

And then she wondered what part of him might be that vulnerable.

"Yoo-hoo, Sydney?" Poe prodded.

And Sydney blinked. "No, it's not a guy. Guys don't giggle."

"Now, that's not exactly true," Kinsey said. "I once knew a guy who giggled. It wasn't a silly girlie type of giggle. It was more like he was laughing at being tickled." She shrugged. "I guess it's like that for some guys. Supersensitive to the touch once they come."

As fuzzy as she was, Sydney checked to be sure she was on the other woman's wavelength. "You're talking about…"

Kinsey nodded, reaching for her drink. "Their penis. The head, specifically. All those nerve endings and everything."

"Come to think of it, pardon the pun, I did date a

guy like that a few years ago." Poe now had pineapple, mango and plum stacked on her fork. "He loved blow jobs, but he never would get off that way. My tongue was unbearably delicious. He said the pleasure was almost painful."

"Unbearably delicious? C'mon." Lauren snorted, then snorted again for good measure. "Guys think all sex is unbearably delicious. I don't think they could have sex without coming."

"Oh, oh, oh." Kinsey raised her hand. "I read this book once on erotica. And the guy had learned to hold off so long that when he finally let go, he said his orgasm felt like it was ripping him in half. Very sexy."

"Or very painful," Poe added.

Sydney sighed, suddenly wishing Ray was here, instead of her girlfriends. Sexy was sounding very good, especially after yesterday's encounter. "Can you imagine being a man and never having a single worry that you were going to get off?"

Poe double-sighed. "I don't know which is worse. Holding back to make sure your partner comes, or holding back because you're afraid your partner will leave you hanging."

"Why would any woman hold back?" Lauren asked, her huffy attitude at full tilt. "I've never understood that. Unless, of course, her sexuality scares all of mankind."

Perking up at Lauren's tone of voice, Sydney swore she was going to get to the bottom of what was going on with Ms. Hollister. "I don't think all women are as uninhibited as you are lucky enough to be."

"And that is wrong. Wrong, I tell you. We should

all stand up and demand our sexual rights.'' Poe got to her feet, wobbling until she caught her balance by grabbing the back of her chair. "Men should not be the only ones having fun. And, whoa, but I think I'm over the legal limit here."

"I don't think there's a legal limit on fruit, Poe," Kinsey said.

"There should be when you've absorbed more rum than fiber.'' Crossing her ankles, Poe sank to the floor of the deck.

"But back to Sydney's original question." Lauren had obviously been pondering the matter. "Why can't women be the aggressors? Why are men so sexually threatened by a woman who enjoys sex as much as they do?"

Oh, now this was interesting, Sydney mused. Was it possible that it was sex, of all things, coming between Lauren and Anton? "That was a question, Lauren. That wasn't an answer."

Lauren pouted. And, of course, huffed. "Haven't you ever heard of answering a question with a question?"

"Sure. When the question is an answer." Sydney speared another pineapple chunk. "All you did was raise more questions."

"You know, I really hate to be the dumbass here, but I didn't follow any of that," Poe said, now leaning on the seat of her lounger.

"Well, it makes sense if you think about it." Here was where Sydney needed to step carefully. "I asked who here had been having sex. And Lauren asked why women can't be the aggressors. Which automatically leads me to believe that Lauren has aggressed."

"Aggressed is not a word, Sydney." Kinsey upended her rum and Coke, frowning into the bottom of the empty glass.

"Well, it should be." On a roll now, Sydney pried further. "C'mon, Lauren. Time to fess up."

"Yes, as a matter of fact I have aggressed," Lauren admitted, not looking too happy about it at all.

Before Sydney could dig even deeper, Poe raised a hand and said, "Me, too," to which Kinsey replied, "Me, three."

Sydney looked from one woman to the next to the next. "Wow. I'm either impressed or envious."

"Does that mean you and Ray aren't having sex? By your definition, of course," Poe asked with an amazing amount of impertinence for someone having trouble standing on her own two feet.

"Yeah. Time for you to fess up, sister." Of course Lauren was equally bossy and brusque.

"What about it, Sydney?" When Kinsey chimed in, Sydney knew the gig was up.

She sighed. "Me, four."

"We are *such* a bunch of sluts." Pushing back to her feet, Poe fluffed both hands through her hair. "Whoo-hoo!"

"We are not sluts." Lauren punctuated her protest by thumping her glass on the arm of her chair. "We are Women on Vacation."

Funny, Sydney mused, deciding that, fiber or no fiber, she, too, had reached her legal limit of rum-soaked fruit. "Women on Vacation. That sounds like it should be a movie title."

Kinsey was still pondering her glass. "An X-rated movie title?"

"Either that or a documentary." Sydney frowned, realizing she hadn't made any progress whatsoever. "But I still haven't figured out who it was I heard on the balcony."

"Well, that's pretty obvious." Poe's hands went to her hips. "It was one of us."

All four started laughing.

"Do you think the guys are talking about sex?" Lauren asked with a faraway expression on her face.

The expression worried Sydney. She was really beginning to be afraid things for the couple had gone downhill. "You mean sex with any of us or sex in general?"

"I don't think guys talk about sex." That earned Kinsey a pelting of several chunks of fruit. "I mean, of course they talk about sex. But not the way we talk about sex. They don't talk about feelings. They talk about the way it…feels. All that ripe and plump and juicy and suction-as-hard-as-a-vacuum-hose talk."

"Vacuum hose, my ass." Poe was winding up into rare Poe form. "I, for one, think we should act just like guys and talk about all that hard and swollen stuff. I mean, does anything feel better than getting your hands on a really hard body? All those muscles and ripples and bulges?"

"Yum-yum." Kinsey clapped. "That really did sound like something a guy would say. Good job, Poe."

Sydney was starting to have way too much fun due to way too much rum. "I watched the guys playing beach Frisbee the other day. Unbelievable. Y'all should've gotten a look at those pecs and abs in action. Talk about drool!"

"Ooh, ooh." Kinsey hopped up and down in her seat. "Naked beach Frisbee. Now that's something I would love to see."

"I don't know," Lauren groused. "I'd think there'd be a lot of stuff wobbling around."

"But we're thinking like guys here, remember?" Sydney said. "Don't they like to watch body parts bounce?"

"They must because they do that bug-eyed thing any time they see a breast move." Poe took hold of the strings of her bikini top and set her chest to bouncing.

"Oh, no kidding," Lauren said, filling her glass again with even more rum and less Coke than before. "I think they prefer a good jiggle beneath a sweater more than a set of twirling pasties."

"I don't know." Kinsey shook her head. "Have you ever seen a group of guys at a strip club? They definitely seem to be under the impression that the less clothing, the more skin and, as much twirling they can get, the better."

"And how many strip clubs have you been to?" Sydney asked.

Kinsey's perky little nose went up in the air. "Enough to know I could do a better pole dance than half the strippers I've seen."

"C'mon, sweetie. Let's do it." Poe stepped up onto the seat of the cedar lounger and began to shake her booty to the reggae rhythm, a rhythm that called for more of a figure-eight swivel than anything.

Sydney rescued the platter of fruit, the bottle of rum and the remaining soda cans from the table, moving them to the deck beneath before Kinsey climbed on top. The umbrella was open, so she stayed on her knees, instead of standing upright. And then, like Poe, Kinsey got into the music with a sensuous bump and grind against the pole.

And then Lauren was up and out of her chair, dancing for no one's entertainment but her own and taking off her clothes as she did. She stripped off her T-shirt, which left her wearing her shorts and a teeny-weeny bikini top, and twisted the material into a rope she worked down her back to her rump, then slid back and forth between her legs. All the while she tossed her head, her hair slapping back and forth like a braided whip.

Sydney looked from one to the other to the next, all three of her friends exuding enough sexuality to seduce the entire western Caribbean's male population. Getting to her feet, she sighed.

If she couldn't beat 'em, she might as well join 'em.

RETURNING FROM AN EVENING spent fishing the north end of the island with Menga Duarte as their guide, Ray followed Anton, Doug and Jess along the path from the boat dock to the villa. Menga had taken the catch to Auralie to be cleaned and prepared for a late dinner.

Ray had spent a good part of the fishing trip discussing housing options with Anton and Doug. Houston's real-estate market was hot with available spaces in dozens of prime locations around the city.

Ray still wasn't sure if he wanted to buy loft space in one of the downtown area's renovated buildings similar to Lauren Hollister's. Or if he preferred to explore the possibilities of a place in one of the historic wards, like the house where Eric Haydon lived with Chloe Zuniga.

Sydney lived in a Galleria area high-rise, complete with doorman and all the amenities. It wasn't Ray's scene, but Sydney certainly fit with the elegant surroundings. Ray was more a suburban kind of guy. Not necessarily the white-picket-fence type, but he liked the idea of sitting on a porch swing and watching the neighborhood kids play.

He couldn't exactly picture Sydney sitting beside him. And that was okay. He wasn't looking to spend his life with Sydney Ford. He wasn't looking to do any more than enjoy her as a woman.

Just as he wasn't looking to do any more than staying alive, making it through every mission he was called out for, minimizing collateral damage by getting in, getting the job done and getting himself and any victims out in one piece.

That was the determination that drove him. And that would keep him out of trouble here on Coconut Caye. He knew well how to cover his backside. How to go into dangerous situations and emerge whole. Sydney Ford had the potential for causing a man serious distraction. Ray had been forced to learn to be indistractable.

And a good thing, too, considering the sight that greeted the four men after climbing the stairs to the sundeck on top of the villa. It wasn't the scenery, though the gorgeous sunset and expanse of tropical foliage in one direction, the wide Caribbean sea in the other, sure made a hell of a backdrop for the four half-naked dancing women.

The group could've put any men's club strip show to shame. Ray had been the first one to climb the circular staircase to the villa's roof. And now Jess came to a sudden stop on his right, Anton on his left. Doug nearly plowed into Ray's back before barging between him and Jess and coming to a halt.

The music that had drawn them up to the sundeck was blaring from speakers mounted in weatherproof boxes in the four corners of the railing. Bob Marley singing "No Woman, No Cry." A sexy haunting sound that set an intoxicating mood. The scents of citrus and female bodies and rum hung in the air. He hadn't had a thing to drink, but was well on his way to being wasted.

Poe stood on the seat of one of the loungers, her arms raised over her head, her head cast down, her hips swiveling in a belly dance made even more exotic by the low-slung sarong pants tied beneath her hipbones and showing off a helluva lot of her ivory skin. Her bikini top, in a matching peacock blue, barely covered her impressively visible assets. Off to Ray's side, Jess made a strangled sound.

Kinsey was on her knees in the center of the cedar table, her pelvis thrust against the umbrella pole, her thighs on either side, doing exactly what she looked like she was doing. A pole dance. With her head tossed back, her shoulder-length hair nearly brushed the soles of her bare feet. Her eyes were closed, her face wearing an expression as sensual as her skimpy red thong and bandeau top. Doug, on Ray's other side, struggled to breathe.

Lauren was stripping, wearing what Ray supposed was a swimsuit but looked a lot more like underwear.

She had her eyes closed and was running her palms over her body, the tip of her tongue caught between her teeth as she worked at her self-seduction. Anton didn't even move.

And then there was Sydney. God, Sydney. She wore almost nothing. Scraps of butterscotch-colored fabric that Ray could easily have seen a stripper wear. A shimmery, glittery two-piece suit that covered her completely, leaving as much to the imagination as it revealed. And what it revealed was plenty, yet nowhere close to enough for Ray's tastes.

And what she was doing was an amazing lap dance, even though she was doing it for an empty chair. She had one foot propped on the back of her chair as she thrust her lower body forward in a circular motion. As he looked on, she moved her foot to the seat, then to the deck and placed both hands on the chair arms and leaned forward.

The motion, of course, lifted her bottom Ray's direction, and he didn't like it at all that the other three guys were getting a look at what belonged to him. He growled, a sound that felt as if it came straight from his balls. He had to stop himself from crossing the deck and wrapping her up in his shirt and hauling her off to bed.

"You know, boys—" Doug draped one arm around Jess's shoulders, the other around Ray's and gave Anton an inclusive nod "—I believe we have died and gone to heaven."

Ray didn't know about the others, but he was in some kind of private hell.

9

"I REALLY LIKE the area where Eric and Chloe are living," Ray said, fielding a barrage of questions from Anton about several of the properties they'd toured before leaving Houston for Coconut Caye.

The eight vacationers were gathered around the dining table, finally eating the fish the men had caught yesterday evening, the fish they'd looked forward to feasting on at the end of their outing twenty-four hours ago.

And they would've done just that if, by the time Auralie arrived at the villa to prepare the meal, the women had been in any condition to eat. They hadn't. To a one they had passed out after what had apparently been a hedonistic afternoon spent indulging in booze and sex.

Or sex talk, anyway, judging by the comments made once Ray and the others had crashed their private dance party.

He still hadn't figured out how they'd ended up being the bad guys when they hadn't even been around for the bitch session. But the women hadn't wasted any time letting them know that men were dicks, or men had dicks, or whatever.

Sitting here now in the company of the same four females, this time all sober and oblivious to most of what had gone on, Ray gave up trying to make sense out of any of them.

After last night's unexpected floor show had ground to a halt, Ray had pulled Sydney down into one of the loungers, settled her backside between his legs and forced her to lean back against his chest while she prattled on about multiple orgasms.

Kinsey and Doug and Jess and Poe had tackled the circular staircase back down into the villa's main room. Ray had decided he didn't want to risk Sydney breaking her neck or breaking his. Besides, he liked having her in his lap.

Anton had dragged Lauren and two chairs closer to the railing where they'd sat side by side without speaking. Lauren had taken the bottle of rum with her and had been the first to fall asleep. Sydney had followed soon after.

Only then had Ray headed to his bedroom for blankets and pillows and a quick shower. On his way through the main room, he'd found Poe and Kinsey crashed on the sectional while Doug and Jess raided the kitchen under Auralie's watchful eye.

Smelling more like man and less like fish, his arms full of bedding, Ray had made his way back to the staircase, only to end up having to wait for Anton to make the climb down, a passed-out Lauren hanging limply over his shoulder.

The look in the other man's eye had been crushing, a sad sort of resignation. It looked to Ray like the couple had had all the togetherness they could take.

Once back on the deck, Ray had used the cushions from the loungers as a bed. And then he'd slept beneath the starry tropical sky with Sydney in his arms.

Her body, bared as it was in that nothing of a swim-suit, had been cool, her skin smooth beneath the gooseflesh raised by the night's soft breeze.

But then she'd moved in close to his much larger body, where she'd absorbed his heat, and her skin had taken on the texture of satin. Or silk. Ray didn't know his fabrics.

What he did know was that he could get used to the way she felt, the way her backside fit so perfectly into his lap, the way her coconut-scented hair, lying there on the pillow between them, tickled his nose, the way *he* felt when she slept in his arms.

Except for that last little deviation from his rules of involvement, it ranked right up there as one of the best nights of his life. Of course in the morning, like a wrench thrown into any good chick flick, when he'd woken up she'd been gone.

He'd lain there for a good long while, listening to the squawking gulls and the softly rolling surf and the sounds of his co-vacationers stirring in the villa be-low. And he'd wondered how he was supposed to separate what he'd shared here with Sydney from what circumstances would allow him to share with her back home.

In one way, this vacation had been a good thing, giving him more than Patrick's disappearance to con-nect with the Caribbean. The two experiences—the trip with Patrick, the trip with Sydney—couldn't have been any farther apart on the pain-and-pleasure scale. But both delivered their own emotionally gut-busting punch.

He'd learned to live with the one; he would learn to live with the other. First things first, however. He needed to figure out where it was he was going to live. When he'd moved back to Houston, his parents had told him the family home was his. And to do with it what he wished, because they wouldn't be coming back. He knew their decision had to do with Patrick. He knew that because, even two years after Patrick's disappearance, they still hadn't packed up his room.

Ray had been in the house a year now. He'd packed and stored his brother's things. But he hadn't decided what to do with the house. The memories weren't enough to drive him away as they'd obviously driven his folks. He worried, in fact, that the opposite was true. That he was keeping the home fires burning for the unlikely event that Patrick returned.

But he was bothered more by the possibility that he was holding on to the past and the memories of hearth and home because he wouldn't have anything remotely similar in his future. And now, after mentally going through the list of Neville & Storey properties again, comparing the amenities of each to his four-bedroom, two-story, comfortably furnished and lived-in colonial, Ray wasn't sure at all what it was he wanted anymore.

He finally finished up his answer by saying to Anton, "But, I do have to tell you. I'm still kinda attached to the house I grew up in. Now that the parents have moved to Phoenix, I've got a helluva lot of privacy. Not to mention more room than I could ever need."

"Yeah, and it's gotta be pretty damn close to being paid for, right?" Jess asked, and Ray nodded, watching the other man digging his fork into the flaky fish.

The men were due to head for deeper waters in the morning. Menga had promised red snapper the likes of which were rarely seen. But Ray still had business to take care of with Sydney. And their vacation time was rapidly coming to an end.

They'd had word that the *Indiscreet* would be returning day after tomorrow. It was time to wrap up any unfinished business. Which meant given a choice between going with the others or spending the time with Sydney, the decision was a no-brainer.

Doug snorted. "Who cares if it's close to being paid for? He's young. He's single. Not to mention that he's a really hot property these days. Right, Mr. Big Shot Search-and-Rescue Man?"

Ray rolled his eyes at Doug's ribbing.

Doug continued to rib. "He needs to be living where the equally hot female action is, not wasting away out in suburbia."

"You don't care if he's getting any female action. You just want the sale." Kinsey made the accusation, giving Doug an elbow in the side while she pushed her fork through her spicy rice pilaf.

"Well, yeah," Doug admitted, and everyone laughed. Everyone but Lauren. And Anton, whose mouth appeared to be smiling but whose eyes were definitely not.

Ray didn't know if he'd ever seen two people more miserable in each other's company. Two people who, months ago, couldn't get enough of each other.

It made him wonder what things would be like between him and Sydney a few weeks down the road, if they'd still be on friendly speaking terms, with their fling over and done with and their lives back to normal.

If his life could ever get back to normal now that he'd seen what he'd been missing the past eight years.

Ray grimaced. "If I decide to sell, Neville & Storey will get the commission. Trust me on that."

"You won't hear the end of it otherwise." Doug delivered his ultimatum with the end of his fork pointed at Ray, then jerked a thumb in Anton's direction. "And Neville over there's going to back me up on this."

"Wait a minute." Sydney looked from Doug to Anton and back again. Her eyes flashed and the glare she delivered was not altogether a joke.

"You, Neville, and you, Storey. Let the man decide for himself where he wants to live and who actually deserves to get paid a commission. You all might play soccer together, but that doesn't mean Neville & Storey is the best firm to sell his family home. Especially when he's not sure he wants to move."

Ray liked it that she came to his defense. He liked it a lot and gave her a quick wink to tell her so. "Don't worry. I'm not that easy."

Eyes rolling, Sydney slumped back in her chair and crossed her arms. "Yeah, yeah, I know. Mr. Big Shot Search-and-Rescue Man can take care of himself.

"I don't know," Poe said, tossing her napkin onto the center of her empty plate and stretching her arms high overhead. "From the tales Sydney told last night, sounds to me like you're pretty easy."

Ray's brow went up and Sydney's went down as she turned to Poe. "What tales did I tell last night? And, even if I did tell tales," she went on, warming to the subject, "I guarantee that you were in no condition to correctly remember any of what I was in no condition to say."

"I remember enough. Or close enough. I think," Poe said, but frowned as she did.

This time Kinsey chimed in. "Yes, but do you remember what you said about Jess?"

"What about Jess?" Jess asked, and Doug added, "Yeah. What about Jess? And what about me? I'm gonna feel really left out if no one said anything about me."

But before anyone could answer any of the questions on the floor, Lauren shoved back her chair so hard it fell over, turned, hair flying, stomped from the room and out the front door. Her feet pounded across the veranda and down the steps. Everyone's gaze turned to Anton, who only stared at the last bite of fish in his plate.

Ray sought out Sydney's gaze and she responded with a helpless sort of shrug. And since no one seemed to know what to say and the atmosphere grew tense, Ray wasn't a bit surprised when Anton left the table, as well, heading for the rooftop deck, not out to the beach after Lauren.

Poe was the next to get to her feet, welcoming Jess's offer of help in clearing the dishes from the table. The two worked quietly, efficiently, and it was finally Kinsey who spoke into the room's oppressive silence.

"I don't mean to talk out of turn or behind anyone's back, but I cannot believe those two are having such a hard time getting things together."

"Some couples never get things together," Poe answered, scraping the leftovers from all the plates onto one. "For a lot of valid reasons."

The comment made Ray wonder if Poe was talking about Lauren and Anton or about herself. And then he looked at Sydney.

It struck him that they'd never talked about life after vacation. About what they were doing here together in the first place. Besides sharing the sort of intimacy that he'd never expected to share with any woman, but especially not with her. The sort of intimacy that he had, in fact, avoided for the obvious reason that the luxury of a soul mate was one he couldn't afford.

He needed to clear the air. Before they went any further, as friends or as lovers, they needed to talk. He'd thought he could pull off a casual affair. After all, Mr. Big Shot Search-and-Rescue Man had done it often enough in the past.

But this was Sydney and what he was feeling for her wasn't the least bit casual. He wanted her to understand how much he cherished her as a woman, how much the things they'd done together meant to him as a man. Honor demanded that he also make her understand that this island vacation was a fantasy and what went on here would stay here.

"Hey, dude," Jess said, interrupting Ray's thoughts. "We're still going deep-sea fishing in the morning, right? You and me and the so-called team of Neville & Storey here?" Jess grabbed Doug's shoulder and shook him hard.

Doug's hair flopped into his face and he reached up to shove it back. "I'm not sure we should trust the womenfolk to do their bazaar-shopping thing on the mainland without us.''

''Excuse me, mister,'' Kinsey said, gathering up the used drink glasses and carrying the load to the sink. ''But we women are perfectly capable of doing our bazaar-shopping thing without you cavemen along.''

''Hey, I'm only going by what went on yesterday.'' Doug bit into a ripe dessert plum and shrugged. ''We came back to what looked like a whole lotta drinkin' goin' on.''

''And?'' Poe asked, keeping her response simple and succinct.

Doug rolled his eyes. ''And I give up. I'm just a man on vacation trying to get along.''

Poe shooed him away. ''Well, then, get along out of here. You, too,'' she said, extending her shooing away to Ray and to Jess, who had already hustled his way to the front door. ''We womenfolk have to figure out how we'll ever manage going shopping all on our own.''

Reluctantly Ray got to his feet, making eye contact with Sydney while doing what he could to ignore a hovering Poe. ''Are you going shopping tomorrow?''

''I'm not sure,'' Sydney answered, bracing her elbows on the table, her chin cupped in her palms. Her eyes were not the least bit tentative or questioning as she captured his gaze.

And Ray knew they were on the same wavelength when she answered his question with a question of her own.

''Are you going fishing?''

Ray swore all his blood had settled in the lower

half of his body. And he wasn't talking about his feet. "I was thinking I might just hang out around here. I'm getting close to being fished out. Might be nice to just relax."

Sydney pressed her lips together as if fighting to keep her expression neutral. "I was thinking of doing the same thing. I've definitely seen all there is to see at the bazaar."

"Okay, then," Ray said, his heart thumping all the way from his throat to his groin.

"Oh, puh-leeze," Poe said. "You two make me sick." She pushed Ray toward the front door where Jess and Doug waited. "Go play in the deep end of the ocean."

Ray let himself be driven from the villa. He'd said what he needed to say. Tomorrow, once they were alone, he'd talk to Sydney. He'd tell her of his convictions, explain where he stood and why.

And then they'd make love, with the air cleared between them and nothing else standing in the way of their remaining vacation fun.

For some reason, Ray mused, that sounded just a little too simple.

SYDNEY LAY on her stomach on the cushions she'd pulled from the loungers, beach blanket on top of the makeshift bed and hands stacked beneath her cheek. She'd arranged the comfy bunk on the far side of the deck, setting it up between the railing and the two umbrellas she'd propped on their sides for privacy.

Alone at last on Coconut Caye, she was taking full advantage of the solitude to sunbathe. In the nude. Beneath the wonderfully warm tropical sun and the wind that swept over her skin in gentle kisses. Actually that wasn't quite true. The part about being alone, anyway. Because she wasn't.

Ray was here, as well, though she wasn't sure where he was on the island. The rest of the vacationers had left an hour or so ago. The women were on their way to the mainland with Auralie, their sights set on the city's bazaar. And the men were headed farther out to sea for what Menga promised to be the fishing trip of a lifetime.

Sydney knew she and Ray weren't fooling anyone. Their tête-à-tête after dinner last night had been witnessed by everyone but Lauren and Anton. For some reason, having the others know that she and Ray would be spending the day together bothered Sydney less than she would have imagined even a week ago. She and Ray seemed to have settled into a comfortable routine, an easygoing relationship that she'd found impossible to share with him back in the States.

There she'd been busy with gIRL-gEAR, the neverending balance sheets, the marketing and promotion, the personnel issues. She'd been busy dealing with the details for the mentoring program, as well as the details for restructuring should the six partners vote to take on a seventh. She'd been busy trying to salvage what she could of her plans to help Isabel Leighton fund her foundation's famine-relief efforts—plans that Sydney thought had been settled.

And they had been settled. Until Nolan screwed up everything by going back on his word and, instead of helping Sydney, making the choice to help her mother. And that choice, that betrayal, hurt more than anything.

Sydney shook off the thought. She did *not* want to be thinking of her father. If only Ray would show his face. Or, anything else, for that matter. Where in the world was he?

She did know he'd accompanied the men to the boat dock and helped with the loading of the fishing equipment. But the group had left an hour ago and she hadn't seen him since.

Her lemon-yellow bikini was draped over one of the umbrellas. The book she'd brought with her to the deck remained closed. The sun warmed her body through the lotion she'd rubbed into her skin. Eyes closed, cheek resting on her stacked hands, she listened to the rustle of the palm fronds, to the low drone of the sea, to the gulls squawking high overhead.

She listened to the sound of her own breathing and counted the beats of her heart. She heard subtle noises, the creaking of the deck and the *thwup* of the wind catching the umbrellas' canvas. But the one thing she was listening for, the one thing she wanted to hear, the sound of Ray's footsteps on the staircase, she never heard.

And so she waited.

SYDNEY AWOKE SLOWLY, realizing as she did so she was no longer alone. Without lifting her head from her hands, she knew it was Ray who had found her. She smiled to herself as anticipation swept through her, heightening her desire for him. Her belly clutched, her heart raced. She couldn't remember a time when she hadn't wanted Ray Coffey. And so she raised her head.

He stood above her, beautifully naked, his shoul-

ders broad, his hips narrow, the scar on his chest a
scimitar slice reminding her of the type of man he
was. Brave and loyal. Selflessly honorable. Incredibly
sexy, virile. Unabashedly steadfast in his values. A
man she counted herself proud to call a friend, thrilled
to call a lover.

His arousal thrust boldly toward her and Sydney
got to her knees, compelled beyond belief to take him
deeply into her mouth. She wrapped one hand around
his swollen shaft, awed by the way her fingers almost
failed to meet, and then her lips slid smoothly over
the taut skin. He was warm and salty and he shuddered when she sucked.

She worked him with her tongue. Long strokes
along the underside. Playful laps over the broad flat
of his plum-red head. Nibbles and kisses and open-
mouth exploration. Bare flicks of the tip where a salty
droplet trickled from the tiny slitted opening.

Her own body opened, her core swelling and throbbing and seeping. Her response became a painful
wanting ache. Wanting him to fill her, to make her
come. Wanting him because she wanted *him*.

This born protector who'd rescued her so long ago
when he'd been barely more than a boy.

This fantasy lover who'd occupied every one of the
impossibly never-ending years since.

This flesh-and-blood man she'd grown to admire,
understand and love.

Tears stung her eyes and she had to struggle for
her own control and patience and concentration on
the loving task at hand. A near-impossible feat she
accomplished by cloaking herself in pure physical

sensation. The beauty of Ray's body and her own body's response.

She wanted more than anything to lie back on the makeshift bed and take Ray with her. To open her legs and feel him drive deeply into her. She caught the salty scent of her own arousal, even while breathing her fill of Ray's musky essence, even while sampling his most intimate parts and savoring his taste, so unique, so unequivocally Ray.

This was one intimacy they hadn't yet shared, and she wanted to take as long as he would let her take. They were together. They had perfect memories to create. That would be enough, she swore, swirling her tongue around the warmly ridged head.

With a long, low hiss, Ray pulled free of her mouth. Hands at his hips and eyes closed, he struggled to back away from the edge where Sydney knew he hovered.

She knew because she'd felt him surge against her palm while her hand had explored the sensitive flesh between his legs.

She knew because she'd felt him pulse into the cupped flat of her tongue when she'd lapped the underside of his shaft.

She knew because his face was a strained mask as he tapped into deep reserves of strength to stop his release. And even as she looked on, fluid slowly seeped from the tiny slit, a creamy precursor to the burst of pleasure yet to come.

With a final shudder, he shook off the last of the restraint on which he'd been drawing and looked down. Still on her knees, Sydney sat back on her heels, maintaining the eye contact that raised the temperature of the blood racing through her veins. His eyes were beautiful, a fertile living green that gave rise to tender thoughts of how loving a man Ray was.

But this was not about love. This was about sex. Again, she forced the reminder front and center. And so when he dropped to the cushion before her and placed his hands on her thighs, Sydney pulled her legs in front of her, keeping her knees close to her chest, her feet tucked up to her bottom.

Ray was impatient. He wasn't going to waste time in an unnecessary seduction. Instead, he simply parted her legs.

Sydney leaned back on her elbows, tucking her chin to her chest, casting her gaze the length of her body and watching as Ray lowered his head. He opened his mouth over her feminine center, breathing a stream of warm breath over her.

Even as she shivered, she watched. His hands were so big, the spread of his palms so wide where they held open her thighs. If she closed her eyes, she could feel the imprint of each finger. Instead, she looked on, loving the way his fall of dark hair looked against her skin.

His tongue boldly swept from the moist opening, where he thrust inside, mimicking the motions of making love, to the tight knot of her clitoris, where he lightly sucked the aroused bud of nerves before tendering butterfly kisses and the gentle press of the flat of his tongue along the sensitive female erection.

Sydney watched it all clinically, analyzing the physical action and her own response like a strangely detached observer. She was doing her damnedest to keep emotion out of the equation. But then Ray looked up. With his tongue lapping with kittenlike strokes, he looked up. And Sydney knew she was the biggest kind of fool.

Because her gaze met and snagged on Ray's, and his eyes told her that he was having none of this composure business. He was here to make her sweat. She watched his tongue. With her gaze still caught by his, she watched his tongue.

Watched the wide flat surface slide through her folds. Watched the tip curl and cup and wrap around her clit. Watched the blue-veined underside, so similar to the thickly veined length of his penis, as he licked her juices from his lips. And then she began to sweat. To squirm. To sizzle and steam from the inside out.

Oh, how had she ever thought she could make this encounter be all about sex when it was utterly, completely about Ray?

Her head fell back and her pelvis thrust upward. She wanted more. She wanted everything. She wanted him to stretch her wide open and fill her up. "Please, Ray. I need…more. I need you inside me."

It was a finger she felt slip into her. A thick finger that slowly hit bottom and just as slowly withdrew. Again she thrust upward. And this time two fingers slid deep inside, crooking up to caress the pillow of her G-spot while he continued to work on her clit with his tongue.

Sydney cried out. She hadn't known anything, any man, Ray…she hadn't known Ray could make her ache with a need that reached beyond physical into her soul.

His hand played her like an instrument he'd practiced on for years. He knew where to touch, to tease, to tickle. When he pulled away, she whimpered. When he returned to test her with three of his fingers, she thrust her pelvis into his hand.

He wasn't giving her what she wanted and her patience was growing thin. She looked back at him, saw the fire in his eyes as he moved his hand away, and knew he had to feel the heat simmering in her gaze, in her skin, in that moist place where he waited.

Leaning on one elbow, she slipped the fingers of her other hand down between her legs, showing him how best to finger her. She dipped inside, where Ray had been, and made him watch while she gave herself pleasure, to her folds, her clit.

The look in his eyes told her how close he was to taking her apart. Exactly the way she wanted to be taken. She pulled her hand away slowly, separating her folds and showing him how ready she was to take him. And then she braced herself back on both elbows and spread her legs wider, issuing her invitation with her tongue caught between her teeth.

Ray didn't need a second prompting. He got to his knees and, his fist flush against his nest of dark hair, held the base of his cock so that it looked seconds from bursting. He moved up between her legs. She shifted onto her tailbone, giving him better access.

He spread her moisture with his plum-ripe head, stroking up and down through her folds. When he pushed forward, she watched. His penis stretched her opening, and her engorged lips swallowed his thick length, and all the while she watched.

She couldn't take her eyes away from their joining. Ray still held his shaft at the base, and the shared moisture glistened on his skin. Sydney had to touch him, and so she shifted her weight once again, leaning on one elbow while her free hand explored.

When she pinched her clit, Ray growled, a low, rolling sound she felt in her core. When she slid the V of her spread fingers over his shaft and kept her hand there, catching the ridge of his head as he pulled free, he groaned. When she licked her lips, telling him wordlessly how much she wanted to take his ripe fruit into her mouth and suck until he burst open, he couldn't stand it anymore and drove home.

She fell back against the cushions, wrapped her legs around his waist and her arms around his neck and let him ride her hard. She welcomed his thrusts, and met every one with a thrust of her own, digging her heels into his backside for leverage. He didn't love her gently, but took her with a rough desperation, saying her name, along with four-letter words she didn't think she'd ever heard him use.

Her orgasm hit her when she wasn't even looking. The base of Ray's cock rubbed over her clit, the head scraped her G-spot with every deep thrust. She let herself go, grabbing his backside and pulling him as deep as he could possibly drive himself into her body.

Her head thrashed and her fingers clawed and then Ray came with a shudder that rocked her to her toes. She felt the warmth of him coating her inside and rejoiced in the intimacy she'd never shared with another man. An intimacy she never *would* share with another man. This bond was too rare, this closeness one she'd never thought to find.

He was silent; even as he finished, he didn't speak. If not for the warm fluid seeping between her legs, the tremors she'd felt rack his body, she'd have no other evidence that he'd come. "Why are you so quiet? You come without making any noise. Why is that?"

He turned his head so that his lips tickled her ear. "I don't want to wake you up. In case you've fallen asleep."

She smacked his backside. "That's not funny."

"Hey, it has been known to happen."

"Not with me, it hasn't." She didn't like thinking of other women he'd been with.

Ray raised himself on his elbows and looked down into her face. "Oh, right. It's you. I forgot there for a minute."

Okay. He was teasing her. He was letting her know that what they'd just done together was nothing more than the fulfillment of the promise they'd been working toward since their first night on the island.

This was exactly what she'd asked for, she realized, even as Ray lowered his head and tenderly brushed her lips with his, kissing her gently, lovingly, filling her soul with the emotion she'd worked so hard to push away. How could he kiss her like this and let her go?

And how could she kiss him in return, holding him close and intimately, his body still a part of hers, and ever walk away?

10

THE HOUR FOLLOWING dinner later that same day found Sydney in the first-floor office her father kept at the villa, a room into which she'd rarely ventured, and never in Nolan's absence.

His elegantly carved teak desk faced a floor-to-ceiling window that took up an entire wall. A wall, in fact, that was the sole section of the first floor unobstructed by the wraparound veranda.

The view beyond was more beautiful than she had the ability to describe. The palms, the sand, the gentle waves of the Caribbean with caps of starlit white. Wearing a pair of tribal-print lounge pants and a matching halter top, Sydney sighed and wrapped her arms around her body, wishing she could express what the beauty made her feel.

But the eloquent poem she longed to write failed to materialize. The ocean's music that sang in her heart remained trapped there, never to escape. The glorious moon rising into a sky left dark by the setting sun begged to be painted, but was caught, instead, on the canvas of her mind.

As much as she wanted to do all those things, the harsh truth was, she couldn't do a single one. Not with the justice they deserved. And for one very simple reason. Sydney Ford didn't have a creative bone in her body.

Instead, she had Macy Webb to write copy and Lauren Hollister in charge of layout and design. She had Kinsey Gray's uncanny ability to predict fashion trends, Chloe Zuniga's discerning awareness of color and style, and Melanie Craine's technological wizardry.

Sydney considered herself lucky. She'd surrounded herself with women who possessed the skills and the traits and the talents she lacked. All she had to do was reach down into the creative gIRL-gEAR well for any expertise she needed, though none of it was truly her own.

Not that she came to the table empty-handed. She contributed the fundamentals required for business, a linear grasp of the concepts involved, a logical understanding of the required theories an executive officer needed to steer a company toward success. She had Nolan to thank for passing along the genes. And her mother to thank, too.

Had Vegas Ford not pointed out Sydney's creative shortcomings over and over again, she might've continued to set unattainable goals, to strive to prove herself worthy as the offspring of a world-famous artist, when she'd been so much more her father's daughter.

And standing here now, in this room, surrounded by inanimate objects that uncannily seemed to pulse with Nolan's spirit, she had never felt the connection more. Neither had she ever felt so alone.

Sydney leaned her forehead on the window and breathed a circle of condensation, looking into her own eyes reflected back in the glass. She rarely allowed herself to get sulky over family issues. She was an adult, after all. Her problems with her mother had, for the most part, been settled.

Yes, Vegas was a flake. She spoke without thinking. She hurt people's feelings on a regular basis, never even realizing what it was she'd said wrong. Her heart was in the right place, which made the injured party feel guilty for hesitating to forgive her transgressions.

It had taken Sydney a long time to come to that realization and to get beyond the things her mother had said to her the night of Boom Daily's party. At twenty-six, she was no less vulnerable. But she did have more objectivity.

Or so she'd thought. Until Nolan, her father, the one person to whom she'd always been able to turn for advice, for solace, for security when she'd felt as if she was floundering, hadn't been there when she'd counted on his help. Not only had he failed her by going back on his promise of funding for Izzy, but he'd then turned to Vegas.

The same Vegas who had, eight years before, breezily announced she was giving him a divorce. She used the same tone of voice she would have used to announce buying tickets to the latest Broadway musical.

It made Sydney sick, knowing Nolan was wasting his money, building the Parisian gallery an ''artist of Vegas Ford's stature deserved,'' when Isabel Leighton was using her degree in nutritional anthropology to improve humanitarian efforts in famine-stricken countries.

Abstract oils versus starvation. Yeah, Sydney could

see exactly why Nolan had made the choice he had. Her forehead still resting on the windowpane, her reflected eyes still glistening, she gave a huff of disgust.

The man she'd put on a pedestal, who'd been her lifeline from freshman orientation to graduation four years later, who'd been there when gIRL-gEAR was the size of a mustard seed and had walked her step by step through the concept development, had hit a crisis in his life, one that made no sense to Sydney.

He was taking yoga, climbing mountains, hitting the streets in his classic Corvette convertible and leaving his cell phone behind. She didn't know her father anymore.

And that, above everything else, was what was making her so miserable.

Almost as miserable as the realization that she'd fallen in love with Ray Coffey. And that she'd been half in love with him for eight years.

How could she have been so stupid as not to recognize what she was feeling long before now? Or, at least, to explore the possibility that her fantasies had a more realistic foundation than simple infatuation?

Not that anything about her infatuation with Ray was simple. But Sydney Ford did not do groundless, ethereal fantasizing. She should've admitted to herself months ago that what she was feeling was not simply going to go away on any prescribed timetable.

Feelings were not as easily organized and classified as spreadsheets and demographic surveys. And unfortunately she was well aware of her tendency to avoid dealing with emotional confrontations. Look what she'd done after the fight with her mother the night of Boom Daily's party.

Sydney laughed to herself, at herself. Eight years ago she'd known exactly what she was up against dealing with Ray Coffey. She knew him by reputation, and she'd willingly gone with him that night. She only wished she knew what she was up against in dealing with him now.

He scared her to death, the things he made her feel. The passion. The uninhibited desire. The freedom from the rational thinking that drove every aspect of her life. How was she supposed to run a business when she wanted to run away, run wildly through fields and meadows, run her hands all over his body, run until she had nothing left from which to run?

What she was going to do was run gIRL-gEAR into the ground if she didn't call this dalliance to a quick halt. Look at her father, his focus all over the map, his priorities shifted, his attitude too carefree to be believed. If building an art gallery in Paris wasn't enough, for God's sake, he'd been dating Lauren Hollister!

Sydney banged her head lightly against the window, then took a step back from the tempting view beyond. If she lost gIRL-gEAR, she would have nothing worth fighting for left in her life. She'd be back to being nothing but the rich-bitch Ice Queen she'd been for too long—until the night she'd gone to bed with Ray Coffey.

During that one night, everything had changed. Especially what she'd felt about herself. During the long hours of making love, he'd held her close and let her cry over her mother's selfish dissolution of their family. And she'd realized the next morning that Raymond Alexander Coffey was a force to be reckoned with.

He'd frightened her, turned her world upside down. He'd seen things in her she'd never seen in herself. It had been a staggering overload, the physical awakening and the birth of new emotions. She'd been glad when he'd told her he had to get back to College Station the following day. As glad as she was that she'd be heading to Austin the very next month.

What Ray had offered had overwhelmed her. He'd fed her ego, given a boost to her weary self-esteem. He'd made her feel whole, when she'd always thought of herself as missing pieces. It had been too much to trust, to assimilate. Too much to ask of herself to believe in his instincts when she'd known herself for eighteen years. She'd tucked that night away.

And now he was back. Sydney closed her eyes, opened them while shaking her head. She'd had another eight years of time spent in her own company. Enough time to know that loving Ray didn't change a thing. Her focus still had to be her business.

If she lost her career footing, she'd fail all of those around her. And, worst of all, she'd fail herself.

RAY FOUND HER in Nolan's office. The one and only place he hadn't looked. She'd disappeared right after the group had eaten. Right after everyone *else* had eaten, anyway. Sydney had barely touched a thing on her plate. She hadn't even lingered long enough to help clear the table, a task she'd helped Auralie take care of after almost every meal.

She'd smiled at the conversation, but Ray had known even then that she hadn't heard a word. He could tell by the faraway look in her eyes. A look that had caused more than the jerk-chicken casserole to burn in his gut. By smiling, she'd been responding politely to etiquette's demands. Sydney was an expert on etiquette.

An expert, too, on the talents most men considered a big part of life's finer moments. Sex between them had been indescribable. Ray had been totally blown away.

Sure, he might be Mr. Big Shot Search-and-Rescue Man—and he was going to kill Doug for that one— but he did have enough sensitivity to know that, no matter that they'd knocked each other's socks off, what he and Sydney had done together earlier today wasn't sitting well with her.

With either of them, to tell the truth.

Ray knew about women. And he knew about sex. Sex wasn't supposed to turn a man's world upside down; he knew more than a few candy-ass names for men who let that happen. Well, it had happened. And the situation was laughable.

Ray Coffey, done in by sex.

Except, in this case, it wasn't the sex at all. It was Sydney. Only Sydney.

He'd stepped into the office, and now he softly closed the door behind him. He had a few things to say and he didn't want to be overheard or interrupted. The others were spending their next-to-last night on the island on the villa's rooftop deck, searching the midnight sky for shooting stars.

As much as he and Sydney had needed the time they'd spent wrapped in each other's arms and bodies earlier today, now they needed to talk. To use words not meant to arouse or to tease. But words designed to cut to the heart of the matter.

"Sydney? You okay?"

He knew she heard him. Because her shoulders lifted as she drew in a breath, sank as she released it.

And she nodded. "Enjoying the view. Thinking."

She could enjoy a better view from the veranda or the deck. Which left the thinking part. And if he had to hazard a guess, he'd say she was thinking about her father. "Must be about Nolan."

She cast a glance over her shoulder before turning completely around to face him. She was so beautiful. So tall and so elegant in every move she made. Her loose-fitting pants managed to show off her body in ways Ray wasn't sure they were designed to do. Her hair swung when she tilted her head, every strand falling perfectly into place.

He felt like a great big clumsy ox, watching as she seemed to float across the room, boosting one hip onto the corner of the desk, keeping her arms snugged around her middle as she lifted a questioning brow. But even more powerful was the strength and cunning he felt, the instincts driving a man to protect a woman he wanted to claim as his own.

And that state of mind made him feel even bigger and clumsier than ever, because he seemed to be plowing heart first into a mine field, instead of taking carefully thought-out and logically measured steps.

Finally Sydney responded, wetting her lips before she did. "Are you into reading minds these days?"

The softly suggestive tone of her voice caught him off guard. He shook his head. God, the way she looked at him…he shook his head again. "Powers of deduction. You're in Nolan's office, surrounded by his things. And you haven't spent any time in here at all so far this trip."

"Had your eye on me every minute, have you?"

That was about the easiest of any question she could've asked. "Pretty much."

Sydney smiled. "Well, your powers are amazing. But then, I already knew that."

His ego wanted him to ask exactly what else she thought she knew. But he wasn't here for himself. At least not in the ego-stroking sense. This time he was here to discover if he had totally lost his mind.

He gave her what he hoped was a heart-stopping grin. And he winked. "Well, Ms. Ford, if you know so much, then tell me why I invited you along on this vacation."

She cocked her head to one side and considered him from beneath long lashes. "To finish what we started eight years ago?"

Ray's grin began to slowly fade. He didn't like thinking that what they'd done today might be the end. A hard reality to face after sex that had turned him inside out.

But even more than the sex, he didn't like thinking they were finished, because he was thinking, instead, of changing his mind. Of not being finished at all. Of making this a start, rather than an end.

He could see himself growing old with this woman. Relaxing in the lagoon in matching orthopedic floats. Napping nude, hand in hand on the sundeck. Watching the sunset from the veranda as they rocked together to the rhythm of the sea.

His self-preservation skills were strong enough,

however, that he wasn't going to offer up his heart without a better idea of where they stood. "I wouldn't say to finish it necessarily."

"What would you say?"

"I'd say it was more a case of figuring out why that night has stuck like it has with both of us. For the entire eight years since."

"I don't think that's so hard to figure out," she tossed off. "A girl only loses her virginity once in her lifetime."

No. That was taking the easy way out. He wasn't going to let her get away with a quick surface swipe over something that needed a deeper excavation. "Well, it's not like a guy has his to lose more than once."

"True," she said, then pressed her lips together, hesitating a minute, before asking, "So how did I compare?"

He frowned. "Compare?"

"To your other virgins." Her explanation came in a voice with a slight hitch.

He moved farther into the room, making his way to the leather billiard chair facing the desk she was leaning against. He placed both hands on the corner posts and made sure he held her attention. "I haven't had other virgins, Sydney."

"Really." She gave a quirky little frown of a smile, blinking rapidly as she did. "That surprises me. You certainly knew what you were doing."

He chuckled. "I wasn't the virgin."

"Still, you were only twenty."

"Nineteen, actually."

Her brows shot up. "You must've been a closet

erotica aficionado. There are thirty-year-old men who don't know what you knew at nineteen.''

Ray grimaced. He didn't like to think of thirty-year-old men—men of any age for that matter—taking Sydney to bed.

''Actually I was the, uh, subject of a sorority project. A...sex project.'' When her mouth fell open in horror, he shrugged. ''Well, not an official sorority. And looking back, I can see it wasn't one of my more intelligent ventures. But, hey, I was a teenager. Most of my brain was in my pants.''

Sydney laughed. Stopped. Started again and covered her mouth with one hand before shaking off the laughter that was throaty and deep. ''An unofficial sorority's sex project? This I have got to hear.''

Now he'd really stepped into it. This wasn't a story he particularly wanted to tell. ''There's not much to it. I was a lab rat for three of the girls in my dorm. Five months' worth of instruction in, uh, sex. Their experiment was about proving that a guy could be trained right if caught early. Before he developed a lot of bad habits.''

''I see.'' Her haughty air had her looking down her elegantly long nose, had Ray feeling about three inches tall.

He wasn't going to stand here and let her judge him by what he'd done before he'd been old enough to know better. Especially when she'd been the one to benefit. ''Crap, Sydney. Don't look at me like that. It was a long time ago. And it didn't mean any more then than it does now. The girls were just...friends.''

''With friends like those—''

''Who needs to waste time on virgins?''

He knew that wasn't what she'd left hanging on the tip of her tongue, but this conversation wasn't going where he wanted it to go. And he was frustrated enough with her attempts to throw him off-kilter to force her back inside the lines.

"Sure, if you want to put it that way." She pushed away from the desk and moved to stare out the wall of windows.

Ray hung his head, studied the distressed leather seat of the chair before pushing away and walking toward her. He stood three feet behind, planting his hands on his hips and looking off into the darkness where flecks of sea foam caught the light of the moon.

"When I won this trip all those months ago, the first thing I wanted to do was grab you up and bring you with me. I didn't want anyone else around. Just you and me and a week of fun in the sun." From his peripheral vision he saw her head come up, and he felt her gaze searching the reflection of his.

"But you'd made it clear that you were more comfortable in my company when there were others around. Macy's game nights. The gIRL-gEAR open house. The cook-out I had on Memorial Day. So I decided my best bet was to turn the trip into a party."

Sydney scrunched up her nose. "I still hate that we were grounded. And that you didn't get your cruise."

"Don't hate it. Be glad." He chuckled. "Can you imagine what it would've been like with the eight of us at sea trying not to get caught banging head-boards?"

"Funny," Sydney said with a soft laugh. "Poe said something like that the first day we were here."

"The first day we were here, all I wanted was to

find out why you'd slept with me eight years ago.'' He said this in a rush, because he wanted to get it out and get it done with, to move on to what he'd really come to say. ''But I got over it. Even if it was to get back at your mother, I don't really care anymore.''

Unexpectedly Ray found himself holding his breath, wondering what self-destructive part of his psyche was still so perverse as to give Sydney such an opening. And when she blew out a long, sad-sounding sigh, he braced himself.

''It was, you know. To get back at my mother. At least it was at first.'' The shake of her head was as sadly resigned as the breath she'd exhaled. ''You would've had to know my mother, Ray. I can't explain what I did or why without telling you about her. And I don't want to talk about her.''

Ray finally moved his gaze from the beach beyond the villa to Sydney's reflection, the pressed line of her lips, the deep V of her brows drawn together over her eyes. Oh, her eyes. They told him so much of what she was refusing to put into words. Words he needed to hear before he could expose any of the emotion he held in his heart.

And he knew this was the tack he was going to take. ''Interesting, isn't it. First you don't want to talk about your father. Now you don't want to talk about your mother. What's so wrong with your family, Sydney, that you don't want to talk to me about either one of your parents? It's not like I'm a stranger here.''

She glanced up into his reflection, her arms tightly crossed beneath her breasts, anger flashing in her eyes. ''It's not my family, okay, Ray? It's me. I'm a spoiled little rich girl and I expect to get my way.

Lately I haven't been getting it, thanks to Nolan and Vegas."

She'd certainly had her way with him, Ray mused. "You may be rich, Sydney Ford, but you're about as far from spoiled as any girl I've ever known. Talk to me. Leave your mother out of it, if you have to. But tell me what's going on with you and your father."

She snorted. "I can't do one without doing the other. Dammit, Ray. Just let it go. Please let it go."

He moved to stand within inches of her, then put his hands on her shoulders. He was only taller by half a head, but even that small difference in height allowed him to keep his gaze focused on the reflection of her eyes. "I told you the other day that I'd gotten close to your father."

She nodded and Ray continued, "Nolan knew I'd been to New York last year and he asked me how he could help. Help specifically, rather than having any donation he made lost in bureaucratic red tape. I put him in touch with one of the firefighter locals and he got what he wanted. His help went directly to families with the most urgent and immediate needs."

"Never let it be said that Nolan Ford is not a generous man," Sydney said, her shoulders tensing beneath Ray's hands.

He didn't like the tone of her voice. Or the way she was closing in on herself. At this rate it was going to be damn hard to reach her the way he wanted to, the way he would have to if they were going to take this relationship further.

But that was assuming an awful lot, wasn't it, since really what they'd had here was only a fling. "He has been. Very generous. I asked him not to say anything, to you or my parents or anyone, but he's put a lot of money into finding out what happened to Patrick. I never asked him to. I only asked him if he had any contacts. He wouldn't give me any names. He told me he'd take care of it. And I'll always owe him for that.''

For several moments Sydney remained still. Between her silence and that of the room, Ray was able to hear the surf rolling onto the shore. Or maybe he was imagining things. Maybe what he was hearing was the rush of his blood through his veins. His pulse beat with a jackhammer reverb. Head pounding, he waited.

Finally Sydney moved, stepping out from under his hands and returning to the desk. This time she took refuge behind it. All Ray could do was cross his arms and lean back against the window frame.

''I'm glad Nolan's been there for you, Ray. I truly am.'' She pulled out the desk chair and sat, crossing one long leg over the other. ''But that doesn't discount the fact that he hasn't been there for me. Or for Izzy.''

Ray frowned. ''What about Izzy?''

''I owe her so much,'' Sydney said, blinking hard against the wash of emotion Ray saw in her eyes. ''And I wanted to pay her back for being there. Through everything. So I went to my father and asked him to help me fund her research grant. He said yes. Then he turned around and funded my mother's art gallery, instead.''

Sydney held the chair's armrests in a death grip. Her crossed leg had long since quit swinging. ''He told me he couldn't do both. And that he'd gone with the gallery because it made the best business sense.''

Ray doubted she had any idea how much she looked like her father right then. ''And you don't believe him.''

''I do believe him. But that's not the point. The money wasn't supposed to be about business. Which was a totally stupid assumption on my part. That Nolan would ever make a decision based on his heart...but he has, hasn't he? For you.'' Shaking her head, she curled her legs beneath her in the chair. ''The money for Izzy was supposed to be about...''

''About what, Sydney?'' he asked, picking up the thought she'd let trail, sensing that his revelation had just struck a very sore spot he would've done better to avoid. The burn in his gut began to sizzle. ''Buying a friend? Paying Izzy for her friendship? You think you owe her for those years of sticking with you? Knowing Izzy, I think she'd be insulted that you feel that way.''

Sydney took hold of the edge of the desk and used the leverage to swivel the chair until she faced away from the window. But Ray wasn't about to let her off the hook. Not when he had a strong suspicion that he was about to get all of his answers. And that he wasn't going to like a single one.

He pushed away from the window and dragged the billiard chair in front of the desk until directly in her line of sight. Only then did he sit. And wait.

Sydney stared at him for several seconds before giving him a reply. ''No, Ray. The money was not about buying or paying for a friend. It was supposed to be about showing appreciation. And about giving back to someone who'd given so much to me. Not out of guilt or duty or any other narcissistic reason, but out of friendship. And love.''

''Is that why you slept with me then? To show me your appreciation? I made sure the cops didn't catch you drinking. Oh, I also held you while you cried about your parents' divorce. Damned if I didn't even take care to make sure your first time would be one you'd want to remember.''

Ray knew he sounded bitter; he hated that any emotion at all had crept into his voice. Especially since he'd just told her he'd gotten over wondering why she'd given him her virginity. Obviously he was the one with the narcissistic ego needing to be stroked. And how sick was that?

''I'm not going to talk about sleeping with you, Ray. Not about then or about now.'' Chin in the air, Sydney laced her hands together. Her elbows rested on the arms of the chair. And as Ray watched, her expression took on the look of new resolve. ''But for the sake of fairness, I'll be as honest with you as you've been with me.''

Fairness, right. That was really what he wanted.

''The first day we were here, all I wanted was to figure out a way to get you out of my system. You distract me, Ray. Seriously. And I have too much at stake in my life to let that happen. My focus has to be on gIRL-gEAR. I wish it could be different,'' she said, and gave a little shrug that seemed full of a pity he didn't want. ''The company is the only thing I can count on. I sure can't count on Nolan anymore.''

Ray got to his feet. His insides had gone beyond sizzling to seething. His anger was all over the place.

At Sydney. At himself. At her parents and his brother and… He had to get out of here now. "I've seen a lot in my life, Sydney. And the one thing I've come to believe in is the importance of surrounding yourself with those you love, and who love you."

And even as he said it, he came to believe it. He'd pulled away from anyone getting too close, telling himself he was protecting them. Instead, he wasn't letting them protect him from himself. Even a short time together was precious, as he'd learned from his time here with Sydney.

She shook her head and wisps of hair shifted and settled. "I know how you feel about Patrick and—"

He cut her off, slicing his hand through the air and bringing his palm down hard on the desk. "Oh, baby, you don't know shit about me. I'm sorry to be blunt, but we've only scratched the surface of one another's deeper selves.

"You can't possibly know how I feel about Patrick, or about the things I've seen in my line of work, the brothers I've lost on the job." He shoved both hands back through his hair and took a deep breath. "You need to talk to your father. Your mother, too, for that matter. It bothers me a lot that you won't."

"*You* can't possibly know how *I* feel about my father. Or my mother." She flung his words back in his face.

Ray headed for the door, stopped with his hand on the handle. He hadn't wanted to get into this with her. He'd wanted a warm and fuzzy vacation, not a trip into the gritty and all too graphic life he'd led.

But if this was the way she was going to live hers, he wouldn't be there living it with her.

"All I'm saying is that you should make the effort. Because you have today. You don't have any guarantee of tomorrow."

THE NEXT MORNING found Sydney sitting cross-legged on the sand at the water's edge. She wore the most comfortably worn T-shirt she'd brought along and an equally faded pair of running shorts. Her feet were bare. Her hair was twisted into a topknot and secured with a sharpened pencil.

She did not in any way shape or form resemble gIRL-gEAR's classy, chic and sophisticated CEO, an image she worked hard to project. And yes. It was an image. But an image that earned her the respect, the approval and the recognition she'd sought her entire life.

She hadn't wanted anything out of the ordinary, only what a mother usually gave her child—her love, which unfortunately, Vegas saved for herself.

Well, Sydney thought. Here she was all these years later. And she had her damn respect, approval and recognition, didn't she? Her CEO position had provided what her mother had not. Proof positive that Sydney Ford, daughter of the world-famous Vegas Ford, actually had something creative worth offering.

So what if she was the brains behind the artistry, rather than the artist herself? She had still put together one of the most talented, creative teams in the fashion industry. And she'd done it all on her own.

For some reason here in the light of day, that rationalization didn't work as well as it had in the dark of her father's office last night—at least, before Ray had walked out and left her alone. Truly alone. Even immersing herself in her father's things as she'd done—so obviously even Ray had noticed—hadn't been the salve she'd hoped.

She missed her father terribly.

And to top off everything, now she didn't even have the man she loved. Ray had left the island this morning with Menga Duarte. And with Anton Neville. Both men were headed back to Houston on a flight later today.

Which was why Lauren was sitting next to Sydney in the sand.

Her gaze on a sailing craft flirting with the horizon, Sydney sighed. Then Lauren sighed. Then Sydney sighed again and said, "I wasn't expecting them to leave."

"Me, neither," Lauren admitted, pulling her knees to her chest and dropping her chin onto them. "What kind of men run out when the going gets a little bit tough? You don't see either one of us running away, do you?"

"Well, no. But then, we don't really have a way to go anywhere, anyway, until Menga gets back."

"Hmm. I guess you're right." Lauren started rocking back and forth, side to side.

She was making Sydney seasick and Sydney put out a hand. "Would you be still before I throw up?"

"Oh, fine." Lauren stretched out her legs and fell onto her back in the sand. "Now I'm making you sick."

"You're both making me sick." Poe dropped down to sit on Sydney's other side. "But not as sick as those two men inside. You would think they were the ones abandoned by their lovers, the way they're moping around.''

"I am not moping," Sydney stated unequivocally. "I am mourning."

Lauren gave an annoyed huff. "It's not like Ray's dead, Sydney."

Sydney matched the huff and raised the level of emotion to patent irritation. "I'm not mourning a man. I'm mourning the end of my vacation...and the fact that I could've taken Amtrak across the country.

"I could've been sleeping in feather beds offered by the best bed-and-breakfasts. I could've seen masseuses from coast to coast, instead of spending a very long week stranded on a tropical island."

Poe, having sat quietly through Sydney's diatribe, now rolled her eyes. "You forgot the part about screwing your brains out."

"Oh, yeah, that," Sydney said, squinting as the yacht on the horizon began to take on a familiar shape. It had to be the *Indiscreet.* She'd been expecting the crew's return tomorrow. But hallelujah. They were ahead of schedule. Finally she could go home.

Back to her fulfilling CEO life. Big whoop.

Still, she didn't want to diminish the importance of what she'd shared here with Ray by joking about their time together. And so she said, "The problem with my brain has nothing to do with sex, but is directly related to the unholy amount of alcohol I have consumed this week."

"I've been meaning to ask you about that. You've always been a tea-drinker." Having pushed herself back up on her elbows, Lauren lowered her sunglasses to the end of her nose and squinted out across the water. "Hey, is that the *Indiscreet*?"

"If any of my prayers have been answered, it is," Sydney said. "I cannot wait to get off this island."

Kinsey walked up then and dropped to sit on Lauren's other side. "I don't get it, Sydney. How could you possibly prefer Houston over this place?"

That was one question Sydney didn't want to answer. Right now this place was too redolent of Ray. Later she could return and enjoy the tropical setting for the paradise it was. Later, once she'd worked Ray Coffey out of her system.

Sydney snorted in self-disgust. Maybe in another lifetime. "I have a lot of work to get back to, that's all."

"Right. I can believe that. All of us here can't wait to get back to work." Poe slanted Sydney a give-me-a-break look. "Of course, I'm only saying that because you're the boss."

"Why does *that* not surprise me?"

"Uh, Sydney?" Lauren's voice hovered on the question. "During all the repairs, do you think the crew forgot to load the dinghy back onto the yacht?"

"Why would you think something like that?" Sydney asked.

"Because someone is obviously swimming toward shore," Lauren replied.

Sydney looked up, as did the others, and saw that the yacht was now anchored in the keel-deep water, and someone was indeed swimming toward shore. Her gaze followed the swimmer's approach until he found himself close enough to wade the rest of the way to the beach.

He shook the water from his hair and his face, slicking his hair back with his palms. He wore no shirt; his swim trunks were knee-length and a plain navy blue with white drawstrings and trim. Sydney figured they bore a designer label because that was all her father ever wore.

Nolan Ford raised a hand in greeting.

Getting to her feet, Sydney settled her hands on her hips.

Kinsey stood, as well, and waved in return.

Lauren scrambled up, shaded her eyes with one hand and waved with the other. "Hey, Nolan. What a surprise!"

Poe was the last to stand. Nolan drew closer, the water at his knees, then his shins, then his ankles. He was out of the water and on the hard-packed sand when she blew out a long, low she-wolf whistle.

"Hel-lo, Daddy."

11

"WHAT ARE YOU DOING here?" Sydney demanded.

"It's my yacht. My island."

Nolan Ford's brows had drawn together, creating a deeply creased V above the bridge of his nose. His dark hair was plastered to his scalp, and water dripped down his forehead and temples to run the length of his neck.

"You're my daughter. I think I'm entitled to show up without having to sit through your third degree."

He wasn't sitting anywhere. He was standing on the end of the villa's private pier, which was as far as he and Sydney had made it after walking off down the beach, leaving Lauren, Kinsey and Poe on their own.

Sydney, on the other hand, was still walking. Pacing, actually. A short strip of planking, back and forth, back and forth, her frustration at an all-time high.

In a span of less than twenty-four hours, she'd been forced into two confrontations, each with one of the two men who meant the most to her.

No. This was definitely not her idea of a vacation. Not in any sense of the word.

"Okay, then. *Sans* the third degree. What are you doing here?" It didn't matter that seeing him had made her realize she missed him. A big part of her still hadn't let go of the betrayal she felt.

His hands were on his hips, and his head was cocked to one side as he watched her pace. He waited until she'd tired of not getting anywhere before he said what he'd obviously been waiting to say.

"You need to go see your mother, Sydney."

If she hadn't already been standing still, she would've come to a feet-stumbling stop. "Excuse me?" she asked, crossing her arms over her chest. Surely she hadn't heard what she'd just heard. "Why do I *need* to go see my mother?"

Nolan kept his gaze steady and unflinchingly honest. "Because she wants to see you."

What would've been a pang of guilt if Sydney felt any guilt over her unraveled relationship with Vegas settled like a jagged seashell in her stomach. "And that's supposed to mean something to me?"

"It should. It will." Nolan looked off across the expanse of green-blue sea before turning to face her directly again. "She told me she has a wealth of apologies she needs to make to you."

Well, that would be a first, Sydney thought, even while her heart began to race. Emotion pricked with pinpoint stings at the backs of her eyes. "But *I'm* supposed to make the first conciliatory step and go to Paris."

"She won't come back here. In Paris she's..." Nolan trailed off. The grim line of his mouth spoke of his effort to choose words that wouldn't hurt her feelings.

A little late for that, Daddy, but thanks, anyway, Sydney thought. She went ahead and finished his sentence for him. No reason to mince words, after all. "In Paris she's what? Happy? Adored? The center of attention? Independent? Unfettered by a husband and a child?"

A vein visibly throbbed at Nolan's temple. "She's not the mother you knew. I don't think she was ever happy here. At least, not compared to the contentment she seems to have found living and working in France."

"What?" Sydney mocked her own disbelief. She was on a roll and not about to stop herself from saying the things she'd been waiting to say for a lifetime. "My mother was unhappy here? How could that be? With such adulation for her work? And never having to spend time with her daughter because she had you to do it for her?"

"I spent time with you because I wanted to, not because I was doing it for your mother. You know that, so cut the crap." He dragged a hand down his face. "This isn't about you or about me, Sydney. Your mother was unhappy before either of us came along."

Sydney looked down, pushed her toe at a lichen growing along the edge of one of the planks. "And boy, the timing of my coming along sure did stink, didn't it?"

"I know you've done the math," Nolan said, his shadow falling over her as he took a step closer.

Shading her eyes, Sydney looked toward the *Indiscreet* and echoed, "The math?"

"When you were born. When we were married."

"Oh, *that* math." She glanced away, rolled her

eyes, surprised her father had finally decided to talk about the truth she'd figured out half a lifetime ago.

He stepped right in front of her, then took her chin in his hand and forced her to meet his gaze. "Do you realize that when I was your age, you were already nine years old?"

Startled, she tried to imagine herself with a child of nine. She did *not* want to talk with her father about sex. Even so, she couldn't help but ask, "What happened?"

"I fell in love." He dropped his hand, then rubbed loose strands of her hair with his fingers.

It was all she could do not to turn her face into his wrist and nudge like a puppy seeking an ear scratch. "At seventeen I thought that was called falling in lust."

"That, too, yes." Nolan tried to grin, but his face was a weary map of frown lines and tough negotiations. "Your mother was amazing. As a person. Worldly and exciting and an older woman of twenty-two. I met her during my senior year of high school."

The same year Sydney had met Ray.

"My life-drawing class visited a gallery where she was having her first show." One corner of his mouth quirked upward. "It was love at first sight. Or as close as it gets."

Sydney was having a hard time hearing over the blood rushing into her head. "I didn't know you'd studied art."

"I didn't. It was a blow-off credit. I remember you taking one or two of those." One brow went up, daring her denial. "I don't have a creative bone in my body, Sydney. Unlike your mother, who has a rare talent.''

''For abandonment mayb—''

''And,'' Nolan continued, ''enough sense to hire a consulting firm to develop the business plan for the gallery. I wouldn't have funded it otherwise.''

Sydney found herself biting her tongue, choking back all the accusations she'd held all this time. She looked down, watched the water lap the base of the pier as a strange sense of calm slowly settled.

Nolan went on, ''I think you, of all people, might trust me on that. I didn't exactly get this far in life by being stupid. I am sorry about Izzy. I'm even sorrier that I disappointed and hurt you. But this thing with your mother…''

Nolan hesitated and Sydney couldn't help but look up. His eyes were dark. Even in the bright tropical sun of morning, his eyes were darkly shadowed.

''This was something I had to do. To make sure your mother was taken care of, settled. She gave me a family, Sydney. She gave me you. How could I deny her request for something far less precious and easier for me to give? Please tell me you can understand that.''

Sydney thought she was beginning to. Especially after the things she'd already heard about family last night from Ray.

Still, to actually see Vegas? To actually feel her brief obligatory hug, to actually smell the blend of perfume, linseed oil and paint that Sydney associated with great joy…and greater pain?

She hardened her heart. ''I don't have time to go to Paris.''

"I want you to make time." Reaching out, Nolan took hold of her hand. He laced his fingers through hers. "I'm going back at the end of the month. I want you to come with me."

"So I can see the gallery and she can gloat?" Sydney asked, looking down at their joined fingers, remembering when Nolan's hand had been so much larger and darker than her tiny white doll-size fingers.

"No." He covered their linked hands with his free palm and squeezed. "So you can see your mother and you both can heal."

Was there any person she wanted to see less? Or any person she wanted to see more? The yearning Sydney had ruthlessly suppressed for years constricted her chest. She closed her eyes, wanting to hold back the tears and finding it impossible.

As impossible as swallowing the emotion suffocatingly tangled like a ball of yarn in her throat.

Finally she looked up at her father, her view blurred by tears. "I'm scared, Daddy."

"Oh, honey. Don't you know that she is, too? She's terrified that her independent, brilliant, entrepreneurial daughter won't forgive her."

The intrepid Vegas Ford scared? Of her? "Okay, I'll go," she heard herself say.

"I love you, Sydney." Nolan brought her hand to his mouth, gave it a kiss. Then he opened his arms.

And Sydney returned home. "I know. I love you, too."

Eventually, reluctantly, she pulled free from his embrace and took a backward step toward the villa. "I need to go pack. So we can go."

"We'll go tomorrow." He inclined his head toward

the *Indiscreet.* "I brought steaks. I'm cooking dinner. I thought it might be fun to hang out. Pretend that I'm twenty-something, instead of old as dirt."

"You're only as old as you feel. And you feel like you've been working out." She pinched his biceps hard. "Ray's gone, you know."

Nolan nodded. "I saw him before we set sail."

Sydney nodded, too, and started walking away, then stopped and looked back. "I want to ask you something."

Nolan held out his hands. "Anything."

"What do you know about Patrick Coffey?"

ANTON NEVILLE eased his Jaguar into the parking spot beside Lauren's SUV. He reached for the keys, then stopped and left the engine running. He'd been home from their trip to Coconut Caye for two months now, and his life hadn't been a particularly fun thing to be living. Which was why he was here. Even though he wasn't sure he was doing the right thing.

What a chickenshit. Couldn't make up his mind about Lauren and now didn't even want to get out of the car.

No, that wasn't true. He *had* made up his mind about Lauren. And he *did* want to get out of the car. But first he needed to take a minute or two to make sure he still knew how to breathe. He'd come too far to back out now. It was make-it-or-break-it time.

And breathing would be a good thing to know how to do if she decided to hang him high.

He stared at the gray marble facade of the gIRL-gEAR building, at the huge lime-colored letters visible for miles. Or at least from any overpass along the

Southwest Freeway. This group of women was about as unconventional as any avant-garde sorority could be.

And that was exactly how he thought of the six female partners and their Asian-American sidekick. Anton couldn't help but wonder how soon Poe would take over. He wouldn't doubt if she'd already set the wheels in motion. She was as independent and career-driven as the rest of them. Maybe even more so.

Wanting her own way. Getting it more often than not. Not taking no for an answer and not liking to swallow when it was forced down her throat. Exactly the same way Lauren reacted. Neither one of them resorting to tricks of the female trade. No pouting or crying or underhanded treachery.

Nope. These women were the epitome of free spirits, answering to no one but themselves. Recognizing the concept of compromise, but exercising the option as a last resort. Hardheaded, yes. But softhearted. And fair.

And he'd been a total prick for taking so long to come to the realization. Lauren wouldn't be Lauren if she'd given in to his way of thinking, given up any part of herself because it was what he wanted, what put him at ease. What he thought she should be.

It had been the sex in the Jeep that had brought him to his senses—right after it had brought him to his knees.

Her sexuality had always been an issue between them. An issue for him, anyway. Lauren didn't have a single sexual hangup. And *that* was his problem.

Yet his problem had soon become theirs, because he'd taken out his frustration on her. He'd made her believe that he thought her physical response less about having him for her lover and more about his body as convenient.

The very accusation women had leveled at men since the dawn of time.

He should've realized that, but he couldn't pull his head out of his ass to see. He'd been feeling sorry for himself, instead of getting down on his knees with gratitude for having found a woman other men would kill for. He just hoped he hadn't waited too long to stick his head back where it belonged.

He and Lauren couldn't be more different in so many ways. Too many to count. And he knew because he'd tried. If he'd been smart, he would've celebrated their differences, instead of trying to mold her into what made him more comfortable.

Hopefully he could make her understand. She already knew he'd been raised in traditional surroundings. A loving, family-focused environment, with a stay-at-home mother, a father who brought home the bacon in a really big way and a younger brother he'd had to baby-sit more often than he'd wanted.

What she didn't know was that he hadn't questioned anything. He'd accepted. Because that was the way things were done in the Neville household. What Marcel Neville set down as the letter of the law was not to be challenged, unless the challenger had a really big hard-on for the sting of a leather belt.

Anton had always assumed he'd be his own law in his own house over his own family, without the leather belt…uh, except in the kinkiest of situations. And for some reason, he'd also assumed that his woman, that Lauren, would be as compliant as his mother had been.

Yet ever since the day he'd met Lauren, he'd known she was as strong-willed as he was. And that was a big part of the attraction. He liked a woman who knew what she wanted. Even while he wanted to have a say or, at least, constructive input into the decisions she made and the way she lived her life.

Sitting here now in the gIRL-gEAR parking lot, he had to laugh. He'd been such a narrow-minded prick, expecting to have it both ways. He wasn't his father and he wasn't living his father's life. Or even living in an era with the same social mores. Hopefully, he still had a chance to make amends.

All he'd been doing was driving her away when the answer was so simple. By letting Lauren be Lauren, by abandoning any attempt to keep her under his thumb, he would end up reaping the rewards of being loved the way he'd always dreamed of being loved.

He turned off the engine and stepped from the car, his plan to show her what a changed man he was putting a grin on his face.

A grin that couldn't be mistaken for anything but the low-down and playing-dirty look that it was.

He'd show Lauren Hollister a thing or two about being a free spirit and getting your way.

LAUREN LOOKED around the conference table, trying to gauge the group's consensus. She really hadn't yet made up her mind about Poe. She hated admitting, after spending so much time in the other woman's company, that she still didn't know whether she counted Annabel Lee as friend or foe.

If there was a lingering resentment for the time Poe had spent in Anton's company, Lauren wasn't consciously aware of it. But then, she wasn't consciously aware of much lately. She'd been back at work now for at least eight weeks, long enough to have taken the Fourth of July graphics down from the Web site and implemented the new back-to-school theme.

Deanna Elliott, the firm's first gIRL-gEAR gIRL, was prominently featured in the campaign. She really did have the perfect look, Lauren thought, studying the face in the most recent catalog, the redesign of which the partners had been discussing.

An impish innocence that fit the firm's ideal. Lauren sighed, leaned her chin into her palm and slumped against the conference table. She'd been an innocent imp once. Now she felt like a gullible dupe.

She was going to have to find some way out of this funky mood and soon. She had no concentration, no enthusiasm and, worst of all, no excuses that would cut the mustard with the boss. It was time to straighten up and fly right. Time to get on with her life.

She had a career to die for, a loft worthy of a feature in any interior-design magazine. She had the best friends money could buy, though they all came free. And money for clothes. Closets and closets of clothes. Oh, and the new car she was shopping for. Not a bad life at all for a twenty-six-year-old single female. Even the single part she could get used to. It wasn't as though it was a death sentence.

In fact, she thought, straightening in her chair, crossing her legs, lacing her hands together and propping her elbows on the armrests, it was an emancipation proclamation. She was free to do anything she wanted to do, be anyone she wanted to be. And that was exactly the outlook on life she would have from this day forward.

Her determination renewed, her attitude adjusted, she pulled her attention back to the meeting, hoping she could infer from the partners' comments what it was that Sydney had just said. Something about gUIDANCE gIRL. And Chloe leaving gRAFFITI and gADGET gIRL. And that the floor was now open for discussion about promoting Poe to vice president of cosmetics and accessories. A seventh partner. Lauren had to make up her mind on this. And now…

There was a brisk knock on the conference-room door at the same time it swung open behind her, drawing everyone's attention away from the subject on the table. The talking stopped. Eyes widened. Macy covered her mouth with her fist and lightly coughed. Frowning, Lauren shifted in her chair and turned around.

"Excuse me, ladies."

Anton Neville strode into the room, not bothering to wait for the excusing he'd asked for. And Lauren was so glad she'd just had her talk with herself, because if not, she might have thrown herself in offering at his feet.

He looked like the sun god she'd thought him the first time he'd walked up and said hello. Today he wore linen pants that were the white-gold of a wheat field and a dress shirt the color of aged tobacco. His shoes were an Italian-leather, tasseled, slip-on design and his tie was wildly patterned in dark greens and browns.

His hair and his complexion spoke of his devotion to summer. Lauren didn't think she'd ever seen his hair so long or so blond, his curls so unruly or falling so seductively down the back of his neck. Even though she'd just convinced herself she didn't need him in her life, he was a sight for her very sore eyes and sore heart.

And then he was across the room and his long fingers were wrapped around her wrist and he was urging her to her feet. His eyes glittered as he captured her with his gaze. She couldn't summon the willpower to pull free from his urgent hold.

"Sydney?" Lauren quickly glanced toward the head of the table. "Do you mind if I step out for a moment?"

"Go, go." Sydney made a shooing motion, which everyone else at the table mimicked, until the entire room was awash in "Get out of here," "Go on," "Get, get, get," and "Don't come back until you finish this thing one way or the other."

The chorus of voices sending her on her way could be heard the length of the executive hallway. The final directive from Macy was the loudest of all. Lauren wasn't sure whether to be insulted or flattered by the group's fixation on her love life. But she didn't have time to dwell on the subject. She was too caught up by what Anton was making her feel.

What she felt like was a piece of property being dragged along behind her master. No will of her own. Subject to his whims. Powerless to voice an objection for fear of reprisal. The strangely sensual submissive role sent thrilling jolts to every one of her body's nerve endings. She couldn't believe what was happening or the way her heart wildly raced.

Under more than one curious gaze, they reached the door to her office. The applause she heard from the hallway before Anton closed the door added shivers to the tingles firing along her nerves.

By the time Anton pushed the door closed and stalked her across the office, backed her up against the edge of her desk and trapped her with both hands planted on either side of her hips, her stomach was churning, her knees were ready to buckle, and her panties were way beyond damp.

The hard wood of the desk bit into the backs of her thighs. The heat of Anton's body raised the temperature of her skin, even through the denim jumper she wore over an orange tube top. She tried a calming breathing routine to settle her anxiety, but with Anton so close, she accomplished nothing but ensuring his scent filled her nostrils.

"What are you doing here?" she asked, even though his expression made the answer obvious. His eyes were on fire, his nostrils flared, his skin flushed with arousal. Lauren crossed her arms over her middle and tightened both hands into fists.

Anton smiled. His lips parted as he stepped in close and lowered his head. He nuzzled his mouth along her hairline, making his way to her ear, blowing a soft stream of breath and whispering, "I'm here for you."

Her breasts swelled, her nipples puckered, and heat pooled between her legs. It was so incredibly unfair that her body ruled her mind when it came to her relationship with this man. But then, they didn't have a relationship, did they?

Which meant it was time for her mind to take charge.

She lifted her chin. "What part of me, exactly, are you here for? Because I'm not sure I have anything left to give you."

His hands moved from the desk to her hips and he slid his palms up her body. When he reached her rib cage, he moved on to her elbows, skimming his way over the gooseflesh pebbling her bare arms and shoulders.

Then he caressed her throat and cupped her face in his hands. "All of you, Lauren. I want all of you. I want your body. I want your love. I want your incredibly sexy, creative, intelligent mind. I want you forever." He lowered his mouth to hers and whispered against her lips, "I want you now. I want you to marry me."

To say she was speechless was an understatement. Lauren couldn't even breathe. She pulled back, giving herself the room she needed to look into Anton's eyes. What she saw soothed her every raw feeling, answered her every prayer, filled her heart with a perfect peace, her soul with absolute joy.

"I love you, Lauren. Forever."

She closed her eyes, opened them, blinked back the tears emotion demanded she shed. "Oh, yes. Yes. Yes, I love you. Yes, I want me to marry you, too."

And when her office door burst open and the room filled with five eavesdropping partners and a dozen other cheering gIRL-gEAR staff members, Lauren buried her face in the shoulder of the man she loved.

12

SYDNEY SAT BEHIND the wheel of her Lexus while the car idled at the stop sign. The Memorial-area neighborhood was suffering from the drought of the hot Houston summer. Lawn sprinklers fizzed and hissed, spraying the dying grass with the moisture it needed to limp through the rest of the season.

She needed to make a left turn. She could see Ray's two-story colonial from here. Four from the corner, gunmetal-gray brick, columns and shutters both painted a pale dove-gray. His shiny black pickup was parked in the circular front drive.

He had to have close to three thousand square feet. It was a hell of a big house for one single man.

Sydney wondered how he'd feel about sharing it with a woman.

With her.

She had no idea what sort of reception she'd receive, showing up unannounced the way she was. She'd only seen him once since their return from Coconut Caye and before her departure for Paris. He'd shown up late at Eric and Chloe's Fourth of July barbecue and pool-christening party. But he had shown up.

Sydney had been sitting with Melanie on the concrete skirt at the deep end of the pool. Legs dangling in the water, she'd been filling in Mel on the details of the cruise gone bad and Jess's island behavior, leaving out his playtime with Poe.

Poe had admitted to having sex, but sex based on Sydney's loose definition, which could mean just about anything from sharing hot, open-mouth kisses to an under-the-covers, snog-and-tickle session.

And Sydney hadn't wanted Melanie looking for trouble where none existed. Especially since Jess hadn't been at the party to defend himself. But then, neither had Poe. Kinsey and Doug had been there, splashing in the pool like two kids. But they were the only couple to have survived the vacation.

Sydney herself had barely survived the twenty-four-hour period after Ray had left the island. It had been wonderful spending that time with Nolan, even as short as those hours had been. He'd shared a lot of his past, things Sydney had never known—or had never taken the time to ask him. She'd been busy establishing her own career, absorbing his advice and expertise, bringing his experience to bear on the company she'd conceived one winter's night in an Austin coffee shop.

But they'd never talked about *his* early years. About the facts surrounding his falling in love and becoming a father at age seventeen. And she now saw her father through very different eyes after learning of the driving fire behind his success.

She saw her mother differently as well, though Sydney doubted the two of them would ever be more than casual friends. Their lives and their priorities were too disparate. And that was okay. They'd made their peace and that was what mattered. They didn't have to make up for the years they'd lost. They only had to go forward from here.

But here, and now, nothing mattered more than Ray.

The Fourth of July celebration hadn't even given them a chance to make small talk. The crowd had been overwhelming and every time she'd tried to get him alone, another of his many friends beat her to the punch. Sydney had finally sat back and enjoyed watching him interact with others, haunted by his parting words from that last night on the island.

He was right. They *had* only scratched the surface of one another's deeper selves. And she hoped to spend the years from now to the twilight of her life learning everything he wanted her to know. That was one of the truths she'd come to accept during these past eight weeks.

At the very least, she owed him an apology for being so cold and unfeeling that last night when he'd bared so much of his soul. She'd brought along a six-pack of Corona as a peace offering. She was hoping, however, to find him open to accepting more. Because she'd also come to offer herself.

The truth of the matter was, the seed of love she'd nurtured for years had blossomed into the real thing. Sydney Ford in love with Ray Coffey. The coldest fish in love with the king of five or six different things.

Who would've figured? Wouldn't their combined graduating classes have enough gossip to last through more than a few reunions…if anyone ever found out…if there was ever anything *to* find out.

There wasn't yet, but Sydney had everything that

could be crossed crossed. Her hopes were up, even though she'd told herself there was a good chance she'd waited too long to make up her mind. And her eyes were open wide. She wasn't going to him wearing blinders or rose-tinted glasses.

And yes. She had something more to give him. A surprise propped up against the six-pack in her passenger seat. A surprise several years, an exorbitant expense and extraordinary expertise in the making. A surprise she wanted to deliver, whether he welcomed her or not.

She found him in his backyard, wearing nothing but a pair of faded blue jeans and high tops without socks or laces. His dark hair was sweat-soaked. His chest gleamed with perspiration even now in the late afternoon sun, and the scar stood out like a bright reminder of the news she'd come to share.

He'd been mowing and raking, cleaning the gutters along the eaves. Suburban home owner chores. And she wanted to help. To work at his side. To sleep in his bed. To give him the babies he wouldn't let himself want. And she wanted to do it all for the rest of her life.

All Ms. CEO Career Woman had to do now was convince Ray that he couldn't live without her. Sydney drew a deep breath and squared her shoulders. She was about to give the most important sales pitch of her life.

Holding both the six-pack and the envelope she'd come to deliver in one hand, she reached for a bottle and had the offering in the other hand when he looked up and caught sight of her. His face broke into an immediate grin, before he had the chance to pull down his emotional shades.

The grin gave Sydney hope.

She handed him the beer. He took it and twisted off the cap. She didn't even try to hide her appreciation for the workings of his throat as he swallowed. She remembered the taste of his skin, the feel of his resilient flesh beneath her lips.

He'd already downed a good third of the bottle when she came to her senses. "I was going to tell you that it's only free if you drink it. But I see I would've been wasting my breath."

"It's good to see you, too, Sydney." Ray swiped the back of one hand over his mouth. "What brings you to suburbia?"

Suburbia. She had to laugh at that. Though she'd originally considered the casual side of her closet, she'd ended up in a pair of sling-back Manolo Blahnik's and a simple boat-neck sheath dress in butter-yellow linen and pearls. Her visit wasn't about fitting in, but about being herself. Accepting herself. Giving herself permission to try, and to fail.

"A couple of things actually."

Her heels clicking against the pebbled walk, she carried the rest of the six-pack to the patio, setting it on the glass top of the shiny black wrought-iron table. Her fingers held tight to the letter.

"Such as?" he asked, finishing off the one beer and reaching for a second.

She looked into his eyes, searching for and making the connection she needed to make. "I wanted to tell you why I gave you my virginity."

Ray paused, frowning, the beer bottle halfway to

his mouth. "I'm over that, Sydney. I told you it doesn't matter."

"It matters to me." She crossed the rest of the patio, steepled fingers tapping the envelope to her chin, making her way beyond the table and chairs before turning back to face him. "I had a huge crush on you, Ray. I had a crush on you for two years. But you were popular and I was a joke and I doubted you knew I existed."

His eyes flared. His fingers flexed around the bottle he held. "I knew you existed."

"Please let me finish." She smiled, tilted her head and held her hands to her stomach. God, she was nervous. And she wasn't going to be able to finish if she thought too much about that look in his eyes.

"You didn't talk to me, except for maybe a passing hello, but you didn't ignore me, either. You looked at me. Really looked at me. And that gave my cold-fish fantasies a lot of warmth."

A flush crawled up Ray's face, and Sydney knew she'd never loved this honorable man more.

She loved that he had the ability to be embarrassed. That she had the ability to get to him that way. That he didn't try to hide what she made him feel. Hope bloomed. Sydney felt it color her cheeks. She felt it in her heart. She felt it until she felt like she was floating. Oh, if this was being in love, she was never going to get enough.

Ray cleared his throat. Twice. "I think we're flirting with the edge of too much information here, Sydney."

She laughed, worrying the envelope back and forth between her hands. "It's true. I slept with you dozens of times before you ever took me to bed. I think even then, as naive as I was about relationships, that I knew how special you were. How special you are.''

''I'm not special,'' he said, and snorted, setting his half-empty bottle on the table.

''You are special.'' She crossed to him quickly, placed her free palm on his chest, moved it to cup his face. She had to do this now before she lost eight weeks' worth of nerve. ''You're a good man, Ray Coffey. You don't have an unkind bone in your body. If the words you speak are sometimes harsh, it's because your honesty won't allow you to say anything but what needs to be said. It was what I needed to hear.''

''I hurt you.'' He wrapped his hands around her wrists and held on.

''I deserved it,'' she said. ''I needed it,'' she added. ''I love you,'' she finally whispered and held her breath.

His gaze snapped up. His fingers tightened. ''Sydney—''

She pulled free from his hold and stopped him with fingers pressed to his lips. She had to finish.

''I've never been in love before, Ray. And it scares me to death that I'm doing this all wrong. I know how to put together marketing proposals and how to design intricate spreadsheets and how to turn a group of six coffee-shop employees into a fashion empire. But I don't know about relationships. I don't know about love. I don't know what to do now and, oh, Ray, please say something before I—''

His mouth devoured her mouth, cutting off her ability to speak. He kissed her. Desperately. Hungrily.

His lips were soft, even while his touch was rough and demanding. He kissed her as if he never again needed to take a breath of air.

But she did. She moved away and gasped, "Ray, I can't breathe."

He wrapped her in a bear hug tight to his chest. "Neither can I," he said before letting her go, setting her back a step and saying, "Sydney Ford, I have never loved another woman in my life the way I love you. I'd say you had me at 'hello,' but that line's way overused."

Sydney wanted to laugh, but her eyes were misty and Ray's were swimming with a liquid emotion. "You had me at 'It's only free if you drink it.'"

He chuckled, a sound that wavered with a wealth of emotion. His voice was still unsteady as he came back with, "Well, call me a guy but my favorite line was, 'I thought you wanted to party.'"

This time her laughter was a cry of pure happiness. She stepped back into his arms because it was where she belonged. Where she'd always belonged. Where she'd never been happier. Where she would never leave.

"So, I guess you've decided to keep the house?"

He hugged her tighter. "Yeah. But living here by myself is getting old. I've spent a lot of years shutting doors I should have left open. I haven't let myself lean on anyone, or need anyone. I thought I was protecting those who love me, keeping them safe. What I was doing was keeping myself from feeling. And I can't be any good to anyone like that.

"Not to those whose lives I'm sworn to save. Not to friends. Not to lovers. Funny thing, but walking away from you made me realize that. Now that I've finally woken up, and now that you're here, I think this big ol' house might come in handy.''

"It just might," Sydney added, stepping out of his arms but only far enough to hand him the envelope. And to watch his face as he read.

"What's this?" He frowned, flipping the unmarked envelope back and forth as if thinking he'd find the answer to his question printed there.

Her heart was pounding so hard in her ears she was surprised Ray couldn't hear it as well. She nodded toward the letter, her voice wavering when she told him, "Just read it."

He absently slid his thumb beneath the flap and continued talking about the house while pulling the letter free. "Yeah. Neville and Storey are just going to have to suck it up. I won't be sending any commission their way. I like taking care of my own. And this place—" Ray looked up into the branches of the oak tree towering overhead, down at the beds of pansies and finally to the letter. "This place is my... own...oh, God."

Ray's voice broke on a sob. "Patrick!"

Sydney stepped away, giving Ray the private time he needed to read the letter. The letter that had arrived by courier only yesterday from his brother who would soon be coming home. One more thing for which she had to thank her father, because it was Nolan's involvement, Nolan's cash and contacts, that had finally yielded what Ray had not been able to accomplish on his own.

And now, watching the man she loved swipe fingers over the tears in his eyes, watching him digest the brief note that promised to explain all later, watching every breath he took hitch hard and catch in his chest, Sydney pressed her hands to her mouth and sobbed.

Ray looked up, his eyes red-rimmed and swimming with joy, and he came for her then, wrapping his arms around her, pulling her close to his body, crushing the letter in his fist at her back. Sydney buried her face in his chest and breathed deep of both her happiness and Ray's.

They held on to one another, loving one another, knowing that, as long as they were always here to offer one another solace and bliss, nothing else in the world mattered.

And, at that moment, Sydney knew nothing else did.

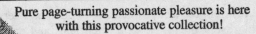

Coming in July!
Top Harlequin® Presents author

Sandra Marton

Brings you a brand-new, spin-off
to her miniseries, *The Barons*

Raising the Stakes

Attorney Gray Baron has come to Las Vegas on a mission to find
a woman—Dawn Lincoln Kittredge—the long-lost grandchild of
his uncle Jonas Baron. And when he finds her, an undeniable
passion ignites between them.

A powerful and dramatic read!

Look for it in stores, July 2002.

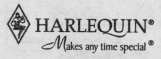

New York Times bestselling author

DEBBIE
MACOMBER

offers sheer delight with

Darling Daughters

Mothers and fathers, watch out! If you're a single parent
and your daughters decide you should get married again,
give up now! Especially if they appoint *themselves*
your matchmakers...

Look for
DARLING DAUGHTERS
in July 2002.

HARLEQUIN®
Makes any time special ®

Visit us at www.eHarlequin.com

PHDD

More fabulous reading from
the Queen of Sizzle!

LORI
FOSTER

with

*Forever
and Always*

Back by popular demand are the scintillating stories of
Gabe and Jordan Buckhorn. They're gorgeous, sexy
and single...at least for now!

Available wherever books are sold—September 2002.

And look for Lori's *brand-new* single title,
CASEY in early 2003